LOVE BEYOND THE WALL
A RIZER WOLFPACK SERIES BOOK 1

AMELIA WILSON

SSPATEL PUBLISHING

STORY DESCRIPTION

Better the devil you know than the Devil you don't. At least that's what they say.

Cara Warden has been chosen by Aldrich to be his bride. Saying no to Aldrich isn't an option. He owns the food source, the water, and the weapons that protect the town from the creatures outside the wall that surrounds the town.

When Cara can't say no and refuses to say yes, she's left with only one option. She'll have to escape Aldrich. She'll take her chances against the creatures who've killed every hunter who's dared leave the town since the shifter pack arrived.

Outside the wall, she's being stalked by one of the shifters. He calls himself Darian. He's dangerous and mysterious. Cara can't figure out if he's trying to help her or if he's just toying with her, playing with his food.

Will Cara be able to escape Aldrich? Will Darian be the creature who spares her or will he be the devil that leaves her to the wolves?

Copyright © 2018 by SSPATEL Publishing
All rights reserved.

In no way is it legal to reproduce, duplicate, or transmit any part of this document in either electronic means or in printed format. Recording of this publication is strictly prohibited, and any storage of this document is not allowed unless with written permission from the publisher. All rights reserved.

This book is a work of fiction. Names, characters, businesses, places, events and incidents are either the products of the author's imagination or used in a fictitious manner. Any resemblance to actual persons living or dead is purely coincidental.

❦ Created with Vellum

CHAPTER 1

Cara couldn't sleep.

How could she? In the morning, she would be forced into a marriage with Aldrich. It didn't matter that she didn't want to marry him. Cara had no other alternative. Not anymore.

She could still remember what it was like before the town had walls built over ten feet high surrounding it. There were mountains in the distance, beautiful sunsets. Back then Cara thought she'd climb those mountains. She thought she would escape her father and leave all the ugliness behind.

People would talk about the big cities beyond the mountains. Cities that welcomed all walks of people, even the new race of people who changed their shape. These big cities still had the kind of things that Cara's mother used to talk about. Taxi cabs, television, and phones that made communication possible across great distances.

The cities who did not fight against the shifters were allowed to carry on as they were. People like Cara's family, who rejected the new race were pushed out of the established communities and forced to build new towns, and ways of surviving without any contact with the Shifter accepting cities.

Eventually war broke out among the shifter cities. At least that was what Cara heard. People left the cities, and so did the shifters. The order of the world forever changed.

Cara thought that perhaps the shifters were misunderstood by the people of her town. She wanted to believe that the world would eventually return to the kind of order it once held. She wanted to believe that the shifters were good.

Then *they* came.

The creatures who walked like men but were not men at all. They were monsters, wild beasts. Every man attacked by them died. Their bodies were brought back in pieces.

It wasn't long after the hunting party was slaughtered that the wall was built. At first it was only five feet high. When more hunters were killed outside the wall, the townspeople added to the wall. It grew higher every year, cutting out more and more light from the people inside.

For seven years Cara, and most of the people of Aldrich Town, were trapped behind the walls. It was a cage, and it was only going to get smaller for Cara when she married Aldrich.

The man was in his forties, while Cara was not even twenty years old yet. Cara knew him to be a cruel man, just like her father.

If it wasn't for Cara's uncle, Mortimer, she might not know that there were men who were kind.

The men of the town angered easily. Many of them took out their frustration on anyone weaker than they were. When this happened, it was up to Aldrich if the person causing trouble got to stay, or was pushed outside the wall to be killed by the shifters.

All matters were taken to Aldrich. When Cara once asked her uncle why Aldrich was in charge he said, "He owns the food. Aldrich owns the weapons. He owns the wall. Aldrich owns the people of his town because without him they starve, are defenseless, and die."

When Cara's father took to beating her, the neighbors called in Aldrich. Cara was thirteen years old when he came to her house that night to answer the complaint. He arrived with a rope, ready to tie up her father because he was not interested in justice so much as he was interested in not being bothered.

When he saw Cara, he entered the home and sat down at the dinner table with Cara's father. He promised to spare him if he kept her untouched by other men.

A virgin.

Aldrich said he would return for her when she was ripe.

Cara didn't understand most of what he'd said, but she knew she didn't like how he looked at her. She didn't like the way Aldrich would follow her home from the schoolhouse after that.

She was relieved when Aldrich married Paulina. Cara thought that since he'd married, Aldrich had forgotten her. Cara believed she was free of him.

Up until two days prior, Cara believed that she would be like every other young woman in town and choose who to date and who to marry. When Aldrich came knocking, Cara knew she'd been mistaken. Aldrich hadn't forgotten her. Not at all.

Her father opened the door for Aldrich. When Cara saw him her body froze with fear. There was a rumor that Paulina died. Cara chose to believe it wasn't true. After all, Paulina was only twenty-three. How could she die so young?

Aldrich married Paulina when she was nineteen. Cara heard people say that Aldrich never let Paulina leave his house. Since Cara's father rarely allowed Cara to leave without an escort, she thought it must be the same kind of restrictions for Paulina.

Once though, when she passed by Aldrich's house on her way to work, Cara saw her. Paulina was standing in the window glaring out at the light as though she'd been in darkness for so long she couldn't adjust. She was bruised, too skinny, and she was crying.

Since Aldrich was the only kind of law in Aldrich Town, Cara felt helpless to do anything for Paulina. Cara remembered that look of desperation on Paulina's face, it wasn't a sight she would ever forget.

Aldrich entered Cara's home. Cara could only think of the terror on Paulina's face. She stood, backing away from the table. Aldrich's brown eyes were so dark they were nearly black as they followed every move Cara made.

Cara's hands were shaking. She fisted them. Cara didn't like the pleased look on Aldrich's face when he saw the clear sign of fear. Narrowing her eyes, she dared to meet his gaze.

Aldrich's cutting eyes widened, the bloodshot vessels in his eyes darkened. His pale face and pointed chin lowered as his heated gaze ran over her. His gray teeth looked sharp as his thin lips curled back.

He pushed up the sleeves of his red shirt. "Take off your dress," Aldrich commanded. His eyes opened wider as he spoke. His hands opening and closing like he wanted to grab her.

Cara looked to her father. He was the only one who could protect her from Aldrich. Sure, her father was hard hearted, and short tempered but he did love her. Cara was certain he would do something.

He nodded to Cara, telling her without words to obey Aldrich.

Cara's face burned with anger at his stab of betrayal.

How can he just stand there?

"No," Cara said.

Aldrich towered over her. He was crowding her space trying to intimidate her to his will. Cara pressed her lips together as they too began to tremble.

Aldrich's hand shot out taking hold of her long blond braid yanking hard and pulling her head back. Tilting her chin up so that she had to look at him. His rough hands groped her breasts as he breathed into her face.

"You need to see who is in charge, don't you?"

Cara was terrified, but she couldn't stand his hands on her body. Reaching up she raked her nails across his face and kicked him as hard as she could.

Only a small grunt sounded before his hand wrapped around her neck. He choked her, yelling in Cara's face as she fought for air. "I'm going to teach you to obey, Cara Warden. You will be my wife."

Her name on his lips was a death sentence.

Aldrich held her up in the air, her feet dangling. The whites of his eyes were bright as he bared his filed teeth at her. His sharp chin stabbed into her cheek as he pressed his face into her hair. He groaned a disgusting sound.

Cara continued fighting for air but wasn't getting any. She kicked out wildly and caught him between the legs. It was all that saved her from Aldrich choking her until she was unconscious, or dead.

He dropped her.

Cara backed away scooting across the floor. Her breath was coming fast and ragged but she couldn't get enough. Aldrich's eyes were crazed with rage. Cara was certain he'd kill her for what she'd done. The scary part of it was that she hoped he would.

Instead Aldrich cradled his crotch with both hands as he glared across the space at her. When he was able to stand upright again he pointed at her.

"I'm going to break you, Cara."

Her father came forward. He grabbed Cara by the front of her dress and hit her hard in the face. It hurt but fear of what would happen next was stronger. The room was tilting as she tried to see where Aldrich had gone.

Is he coming? Is my father really going to hand me over to him? Aldrich's worse than any creature that could be outside the walls.

"I will come for her Thursday," Aldrich told her father. "Make certain she is here and ready for me."

When the door slammed, Cara relaxed. She stopped struggling against the dizziness and gave in to the darkness that filled her vision.

Her father apologized when she woke. It was strange for Cara, because he did actually appear sorry. It was the only time she'd ever seen real remorse in his brown eyes.

"Aldrich will starve us if we deny him. We would both die if I refuse him."

"I'd rather starve to death than let Aldrich take me," Cara told him.

"I know," he'd answered. "But I wouldn't."

He didn't lock her in her room or in the house because there was no where she could go. Nowhere to run away from Aldrich. No one would hide her. If Aldrich found her hiding with anyone, he would starve the entire family.

Her uncle Mortimer and his wife were the only good people she knew. Even though her father rarely let her see them, she loved them and their children. She loved them too much to have them starve for her.

Cara sat up on the mattress that served as her bed.

Thinking of Paulina in that house, looking out like she'd forgotten what the sun felt like, made Cara feel smothered. Even the thin worn blanket on her legs was too much. She pushed it off and onto the floor.

Cara needed to get outside. She needed to breathe in the cold air.

Pulling on her hand-me-down boots, she spotted her shawl on the hook by the door. Cara wrapped it around her shoulders. On an impulse, she grabbed the scissors from the tabletop as she passed by on her way out the front door.

As soon as she was outside she felt a little better.

The air was frosty. Her breath looked like smoke in the dark. Cara breathed hard, like she did after Aldrich choked her. She walked away from her father's house. It was the first time in five years she's been in the town without an escort. It was the last bit of freedom she'd ever get.

Cara walked through the small town finding herself on the main square. Aldrich's house was up ahead. Cara looked up, spotting Paulina's handprints still on the glass of the upper window.

Cara remembered Aldrich's hand around her braid, his face in her hair, and his breath on her neck. Rage and revulsion burned up her fear until it was gone.

Raising the scissors, Cara chopped off her braid at the nape of her neck. Just like that she felt lighter. She knew her father would be furious, and she knew Aldrich would be too.

I'm done being afraid.

The town horn sounded, signaling a change of the guard. Cara spotted the guard climbing down the tall ladder to go report and trade places with the next guard on duty. She watched him with disbelief.

The guard tower is empty.

She'd dreamt of stealing the ladder enough times that as she watched the guard walk away Cara wasn't sure if she were dreaming again.

Taking hold of the ladder, she tried to shift it to lean on the wall instead of the tower but it was too heavy for her. Before she could think better of what she was doing, Cara started climbing.

The sun was rising and the sky above was just hinting at the color blue. Excitement leapt in her chest. She wanted to see the mountains. She wanted to see the field and the forest. Cara kept climbing.

"Hey, hey you there," someone called out. Cara climbed faster. Ten more rungs up the ladder and she would reach the tower. Her hands were wet with sweat and it was becoming more difficult to hold on. The ladder shook. Cara looked down to see a guard climbing up after her.

Faster, come on Cara

CHAPTER 2

"The creatures are out there. You shouldn't be on the tower," the man called up after her.

"They can't be any worse than the creature in here," Cara said as she crawled onto the landing of the guard tower. Her adrenaline was pumping, her heart pounding hard, and fast. She couldn't hear what the guard was saying.

Reaching Cara grabbed the railing and pulled herself up.

The sky over the east mountains was streaked with orange, pink, and purple.

Freedom.

The hand of the guard grabbed the top rung on the ladder. He'd almost caught up to her. He would try and stop her, she was sure of it. Cara climbed over the railing and turned toward the wall. It wasn't a far jump but it was a long way down.

"Wait. What are you doing?"

Cara jumped landing easily on the wall ledge.

"Take my hand, I'll pull you back onto the tower. You don't know what you're doing," he said, his voice kind and full of concern. Cara looked back at him and could see recognition in his eyes, but she didn't know him. Her father kept her away from most of the people in the town.

"Cara. Aldrich's bride," he said. His outstretched hand dropped. "You're Mortimer's niece."

He knows my uncle.

Cara was afraid he was going to try and stop her again. She looked down onto the other side of the wall trying to see a way to escape without breaking her neck.

"I'll tell your uncle that you got away," the guard said.

Cara turned back, surprised by what he's saying. "You're not going to try and stop me?"

He untied a red pouch from his belt and held it out to her. "It isn't much," he said, his face solemn. "Good luck."

Cara was still scared to reach for the pouch. Afraid it was a trick and he was going to pull her back onto the guard tower platform. She was afraid he would snatch away her one chance to escape.

"The… things that live out there. They're dangerous. You'll need this," he insisted, holding the pouch out again.

Cara snatched the pack out of his hand and was surprised when he didn't reach for her or try to catch her.

He really is trying to help me.

"Thank you."

"You should hurry. I saw Aldrich's servants opening the house to prepare for your wedding. He'll be coming to get you soon and discover you're gone."

The ledge was thin, and with the wind Cara didn't know how long she would be able to stay on top of it. Kneeling on the wall she tucked the pouch under the thin bra that was one of the many Aldrich issued articles of clothing for the women. He was the only one with the connections to trade with the stronger cities.

Curving her hands around the edge Cara began to lower herself down the other side of the wall until she was hanging. Her feet scraped the stones as she tried to find a foot hold.

Her right foot caught hold under her toes.

I can do this.

Scraping her left foot over the surface, she struggled to find a hold. The wind blew so hard that Cara almost lost her grip on the wall. She couldn't feel the grooves in between the stones with the boots on. Wiggling her foot, she felt the oversized boot fall free. Her toes ran over the cold stone searching and probing for a hold. Finally, she found a very thin ledge.

"Hurry, someone is coming," the guard whispered in a hiss.

Releasing her hold on the top ledge with her left hand, Cara slid it over the sharp cold edges of stone until she found a place to hold on. Just as her other hand slid off the ledge, she heard him.

Aldrich.

"She was outside my house. This is her hair. Find her."

"Yes sir," someone answered him, a guard probably but anyone in Aldrich Town would do his bidding. Cara didn't blame them. She knew what the consequences were for refusing Aldrich. Cara's hands were starting to shake again.

So much for being fearless.

She lowered herself further down the stone wall, feeling her way as she went. Cara's foot rested on a sharp ledge biting into her flesh. The descent was slow and difficult. Her muscles began to spasm and she had so much farther to go.

"You must have seen her. Where did she go?" Aldrich called out.

"I didn't see her. She must have come by during the shift change. I didn't see anyone," the guard lied.

Cara gained another foot, but it was still too dark to see where the floor below began. If she let go she might suffer bruised feet, or worse broken bones.

Just keep climbing.

"What is this?" Aldrich's voice sounded victorious.

Cara looked up, certain that he'd climbed the tower and was looking down at her. Her hold slipped and she slid down the wall, her nails scraping against the rock, and tearing away. She caught herself with her right hand, her arm jerking hard.

Biting her lip, she stifled a cry of pain as her feet searched out holds and grooves in between the stones.

"This is hers." Aldrich accused. His voice sounded like it came from the tower. He must have climbed up while she was sliding down the wall. If he looked down, he might see her. It was still dark but the sun was continuing to rise.

"It's the same shawl that all the girls wear. It's the standard you yourself issue out to the women."

"Are you saying it's not hers? That this couldn't be Cara's?"

A muffled sound drew her eyes upward. Aldrich was smashing the shawl against the guard's face. Cara watched in horror. She didn't know what to do.

The guard fought his way free of Aldrich, he gasped for air as he leaned over the wall. His eyes were searching the darkness. He was looking for Cara, but he couldn't see her even though she was only a dozen or so feet down the wall.

He mouthed the word, "Run."

Aldrich slipped the shawl around his neck and shoved him over the wall. His pointed face leaned over the wall after he'd tied off the shawl to the tower. "You lied to me. You saw her. *My Cara.*"

The guard's feet kicked, his heels scraping on the wall but they weren't catching. He was choking. Aldrich wasn't going to release him.

Cara reached up, climbing upward as fast as she could. The light caught her hand as she took hold of his shoe and pushed, trying to help him.

"No," the guard gurgled out kicking her hand away.

I can't let you die.

She reached up again as Aldrich pressed his face into the dying man's neck. "Do you know how long I've waited to fuck her? To break her?"

He kicked her hand away again, only this time she lost her grasp on the wall. Cara pushed off from the wall with her feet, hoping to land on the other side of the mote around the outer wall.

Aldrich straightened away from the dead guard, blood dripped down his chin as he cut the shawl and turned away.

Water enveloped her into freezing cold darkness. The dim light from above cast a silhouette of the guard who saved her life and gave his own. He was floating on the surface.

Cara choked on water as she tried to crawl up from the depths of the murky liquid. She didn't know how to swim, but her frantic movements seemed to be working though too slow to do her much good.

She kicked her feet harder, climbing faster. When she reached him, Cara pulled until her head broke through the surface. A deep breath of air filled her lungs. She coughed.

It was so loud, her coughing in the silence. Aldrich would hear her. Someone would hear her. The quaking of her body was so violent she knew her thrashing around in the water would draw notice.

Sharp rocks stabbed into her back expressing what little air she'd managed to get. The force pushed her back under the surface but she didn't let go of her hero. She reached up again. This time her hand caught hold of a boulder.

Cara pulled herself above the surface again. She tried to climb, out but she couldn't do it holding onto the dead guard's shirt. With a silent sob, she let go and climbed out of the still water. Its slimy texture increased the difficulty of climbing out.

Cara's body was still shaking too hard. Her teeth chattering like drums. The boots she'd kicked off were long gone, probably at the bottom of the mote.

She should go, run even, but Cara couldn't leave him like he was. This man who saved her was floating face down in the filthy, still water. It was foul smelling, and with the sun continuing to rise Cara could see human waste floating along the surface.

Cara bent down and took hold of his jacket. She braced herself with her feet flat on the huge boulder and pulled. It was slow going pulling him up the rocky, muddy slope. When she stopped to rest, he started sliding back in.

No. No. Please, no.

Her arms shook with the strain to hold his head above the water. Using all the muscle in her legs she pushed against the boulder gaining another two feet of his body onto the slope. Cara climbed a step higher. She began pulling the dead weight from the water. It didn't matter how many times she had to do it. Cara wasn't leaving him to rot in filth. He deserved a hero's burial.

I don't even know his name.

CHAPTER 3

The wind carried a new scent, waking Darian from a deep sleep. It was a delicious, sweet smell. It was strange because it didn't just appeal to his wolf, he found the scent alluring in his human form as well.

Darian walked to the open window and looked out, trying to locate the source of the scent that called to him.

It's coming from Aldrich Town? Nothing good ever comes out of that place. Hunters looking to kill my pack. The stench of desperation all over them.

I won't stand by and let another one of them try and weed out my pack. Aldrich's men won't take another.

Darian, the alpha of his pack usually kept good control of his temper and the wolf spirit that shared his shifter body. This time he didn't want to stay in control, he wanted to teach the hunters a lesson. He let the wolf spirit surge forward feeding on Darian's anger.

His body began to shift from Darian's human form to that of his wolf. His muscles stretched and grew. The pants stretched and ripped around his legs as they too grew and shifted. Bones cracking and extending his human body changed into that of an oversized white wolf.

The wolf spirit, his wolf, was ready for the kill. He was ready to defend the pack and their home. Darian leapt out the second story window, landing in a run.

Limbs stretching, he charged down the mountainside and into the forest below. Animals raced to get clear of his path. He was all predator. Darian pulled his humanity back allowing his wolf, the alpha of the Rizer pack, to take the lead.

He knew he could trust his wolf's instincts. If it was another hunter, he would die like all the others. No one would hurt his pack, not without going through him first.

The sun wasn't up yet, but that didn't matter. Darian could see well in the dark. He knew these woods so well he could traverse them with his eyes shut.

At full speed, he crossed the sixty acres of overgrown forest in just under ten minutes. Darian slowed as he reached the edge of the forest that opened into the clearing that led to the filthy water surrounding Aldrich's Town.

His wolf found the movement right away.

The hair on the back of his neck and all down his spine raised up as a feral growl vibrated through his entire frame and into the earth under his feet. Darian left the shelter of the trees. He moved along the boulders and rocks staying low to the ground. The hunter was breathing hard, coughing.

Disgust turned his stomach. The hunter bathed in the infested sewage.

Is everyone who comes out of Aldrich Town so detestable?

He knew that he'd taste what the hunter had been swimming in when he killed him. It made Darian hate the hunter all the more.

The path he was taking put him on higher ground than the hunter. Every step he took was silent. Darian was intent on getting right over head of the hunter.

The murderer won't even see me coming.

There was blood in the air. He'd already made a kill and from the smell of the blood, it was one of his own kind. A human. Darian wasn't surprised. He was one of Aldrich's people, why wouldn't they be every bit as blood thirsty as their leader?

He leapt onto the white rock that leaned in toward the water. The hunter had his back to Darian. He was small. In fact, he was very small. A teen boy, most likely. At first Darian thought the boy was drowning the man in his arms the way he kept dropping him in the water. As the boy struggled, grunting, and praying, Darian realized the boy was trying to pull the dead man from the water.

He must have to show Aldrich proof of his kill.

Darian wasn't going to like having to kill a human boy who was still so young. Even his wolf pulled back to watch the boy instead of striking while he was otherwise distracted. Taking a life was no small matter.

Why does it have to be a young boy?

"Thank you," the boy said to the dead man as he finally managed to get his top half out of the water. He was younger than Darian first believed. His voice had not even begun to develop into manhood. His clothes and most of his face was caked in mud and filth from the mote.

Darian grabbed onto the new wave of derision the boy provided.

Is thanking your victim for giving his life supposed to make it okay that you took it in the first place?

Aldrich's signature bite mark on his victim was present on the corpse. This boy was clearly Aldrich's protégé.

Crouching, Darian readied himself to launch. Killing the protégé of Aldrich would hit closer to the heart of Aldrich than Darian and his pack had ever had the chance to strike before.

The boy bent down closing the dead man's eyes. Darian could smell the salty tears leaking from the boy's eyes, and mixing in the grime smeared over his heart-shaped face. Darian continued to watch the boy, too confused as to what to make of the young killer.

His hair is misshapen.

The blond strands were hanging in a diagonal slant from the back of his right ear to the top of his left shoulder. His heart beat frantically in his chest, as though he was afraid the dead man might wake and take revenge. The boy returned to the thin ledge and dragged the legs of the dead man out of the water. He kept looking back up toward the wall. No one was watching the boy who was clearly guilty.

This boy deserves to die. Darian repeated to himself trying to get his wolf to sit right with it, to get himself to accept what must be done.

His wolf pushed, ready to leap. Darian exhaled, beginning to draw back. He didn't want to remember killing a boy this young, even if he was a murderer.

The boy wept heavily as he removed the shoes from the dead man and put them on his own tiny feet. Darian cursed himself an idiot for waiting when he saw the boy pull a silver blade from the belt of the man who was dead.

Shit. I should have taken him before he robbed his victim of his blade. Now I will have to be more careful.

The people inside were rustling about. It was early for them to be up and running around. Something was stirring inside the walled off town. Darian could see from the way the boy tensed that he heard it too.

The wet and shivering bag of bones ducked his head and began to climb the rocky incline. He never once checked his surroundings.

He doesn't even walk right. What is he wearing?

The boy's hurried steps made him clumsy. His clothes clung to him strangely, was he wearing a cape or night shirt? He ran away from Aldrich's Town. Darian could smell the boy's fresh blood as he crashed into a jagged edge on a rock.

He's pathetic. The boy won't last in the forest for more than a few hours. If the forest doesn't take him, then I will

CHAPTER 4

The shouts coming from Aldrich Town grew louder. People called her name, others shouted orders, telling each other where to search. They were trying to keep Aldrich happy, to keep him from punishing them.

He's a monster, a murderer. We all saw what he was doing to Paulina. I should have done something. I should have tried to break her out.

Tears blurred her vision as she started up the incline toward the dark forest. Her chin was the only spot on her body that wasn't freezing. The blood from the cut was warm as it ran down her neck.

I need to get farther away. I can't let him find me.

The guard's shoes were too big. Cara struggled to keep her balance and risked another fall. It was too dangerous. She couldn't afford any more injuries. Stepping out of the shoes, Cara hugged them against her chest as she continued over the sharp rocks.

She was beginning to lose feeling in her feet. The water was so cold, and the rocks were like sharpened ice cubes. She was almost to the forest. Concentrating on the path in front of her, she pushed aside the pain that was beginning to break through the cold.

Keep moving, keep going.

The horn sounded from the town in three short bursts. Cara

hit the ground crawling into the underbrush at the edge of the woods. She looked back toward the town, knowing that the three short bursts meant that there was something outside the walls.

Someone must have seen me.

A guard pointed beyond the mote.

They found the guard.

They hadn't seen her, but when they came to bury the guard they would discover that someone drug him up onto land from the water. Even if they didn't figure out he'd been moved, they'd figure out that Cara escaped.

Aldrich will make them look for me. I have to keep moving.

Just as she began to move she saw it. A giant white wolf running over the boulders in her direction. His yellow eyes trained on Cara.

Shit.

Cara pulled out the blade and pointed it at the wolf. It was too big to be just an ordinary wolf. It was one of them.

A shifter.

Anger and hatred hardened the features on her face. They were the reason for the wall, the reason she and everyone else had to agree to be caged. They were prisoners with a man like Aldrich deciding who would live and who would die.

The shifter didn't slow down. He continued toward her and didn't stop until he was only a few feet away. The wolf stood just outside her reach. His lips curled back showing her sharp teeth as a growl rumbled from the chest of the beast.

"I will kill you. I'm not afraid of you," Cara said, ignoring the shaking of the blade in her hand. It was the cold not her fear. She hated the monster too much to have any room for healthy fear. "You stole my freedom."

His white head turned as he began to pace in a wide circle around Cara. The yellow eyes of the beast were no longer staring into hers. They were running over her body, the head of the wolf lifted smelling the air. He drew closer.

"Not another step," Cara growled through clenched teeth. The wolf snapped its massive jaws together, the clap of teeth against teeth was like a gun shot. She almost dropped the blade.

The wolf leapt toward her.

Cara swung the blade, catching the beast on the biggest part of his thick, white fur covered front leg. The wolf leapt back, the cry of pain surprising Cara.

It's true what they say about the silver. The shifters can't stand to touch it.

A snarl ripped through the air like thunder.

Cara's legs shook harder. She was scared, there was no denying that now. The wolf snarled and barked at her, his rage clear to see.

This is it.

She held the blade with both hands, pointing the tip toward the enraged shifter.

The wolf came at Cara fast, catching her right arm with his powerful jaws. Cara released the blade with her right hand, taking it into her left.

Pain radiated through her arm, but she was used to pain. It was the sight of the blood and the sharp teeth that made her cry out. The wolf released her arm, his huge head rising. His yellow eyes widened at her.

Cara brought the handle of the blade down hard, catching the wolf on the side of his head. A small yelp of surprise more than pain came out of the beast and he shot away into the forest.

She gripped the weapon and stumbled forward.

I have to get deeper into the woods. Aldrich. He'll be coming.

Darian crouched low, watching in disbelief as the wounded human trudged deeper into the forest.

A woman?

He didn't know, until she screamed. The stench of the water covered her feminine scent. The way she'd acted determined to pull the body from the water, he'd assumed it had to be a young boy. What he'd taken to be cape was not a cape at all. It was a dress.

I attacked a woman.

The guilt that poured through him was overwhelming. It shouldn't make a difference. If she was a murderer, then she deserved death just like the other hunters that came after Darian's pack, his family. It *did* matter though. She was a weak, human woman. The skin discoloration on her face was proof of abuse. The woman was misused. She was mistreated by her own people.

The betrayal of enduring abuse from her people, her family, it must be what drove her to murder.

She continued walking. As she moved chunks of mud and the filth from the mote began to slide away from the material of her dress. It was a blue nightgown. What he'd mistaken for large clumps of mud, he now recognized were the womanly curves of a female. The rip up the side of the ruined nightgown gave Darian glimpses of long lean legs.

How the hell did I ever think she was male?

She should be too exhausted to continue. The amount of blood she was losing wasn't extreme, but if the wound went untreated, she would suffer infection.

Darian had to give her credit, she wasn't crying. Most of the hunters cried when they faced him, especially if they managed to fight him off momentarily as she had.

She spotted him a few times as he followed her. The deep frown and scowl she aimed at him should have made him feel resentful.

It didn't.

The woman had spirit, and a brave heart.

She walked for hours not stopping to rest, or to find food. Darian couldn't help but wonder what was driving her so hard to continue. With the sun nearing the highest point in the sky, Darian knew his pack would be coming soon to look for him. He should kill the woman and be done with it. She was heading toward their community. Darian couldn't allow her to find it.

She stopped walking abruptly. He watched her tilt her head and make a turn toward the west.

The waterfall. Yes, please wash the filth from your body. You smell horrible.

Everclear, was what Darian's people called the waterfall where the woman with the short golden hair finally stopped. She scanned the forest line startling when she found him watching her.

"What? What do you want?" she demanded. "Let's fight to the death, or leave me the hell alone," she challenged. Her hands fisted on her hips as she stared at him.

She is beautiful.

There was no denying it. Covered in filth, and with hacked up hair, a bloody chin, and an angry scowl on her face, she was still beautiful. Her lips were tight as she stared at him. She was not stupid. Darian could see she was afraid of him, but she was facing him.

"Well?" she said again.

Darian smiled inwardly. This human thought to boss him around? Did she take him for a pet?

He lay down in the twigs and leaves several yards away, showing her that he did not intend to leave, but neither was he attacking.

She hissed out a breath, glaring at him even harder than she was before. "You're going to wait until I'm asleep? Vulnerable? Why?"

Darian gave her no response.

The woman looked down at the bite in her wrist. Her clenched teeth, the only indication of her pain. Indigo blue eyes landed on him again. "Kill me, don't kill me. I don't care. I'm washing off."

She kicked off the shoes and turned her back to him. Reaching beneath the gown she pulled out a cloth pack and dropped it next to the shoes. Next, she stripped away the bra she was wearing while keeping the gown on to shield her body from him. She folded it carefully and set it on the cloth bag.

Her spine stiffened when she stood up. She stared out at the water. He could hear her heart pounding before she stepped into the water. She was still holding the blade as she lifted the dress only high enough to avoid the water.

Inch by inch he watched the dress climb higher up her smooth fair skin. He realized he was holding his breath as his hungry gaze swept over her exposed skin.

She's so beautiful.

Her breath shook as she exhaled. She looked over her shoulder at him to see if he was watching. The hem of her skirt was just under her ass. Darian didn't want her to stop. His heart was pounding as he waited for more.

"Forget the shifter. Just do it, Cara," she spoke quietly to herself but he could hear her as if she were right beside him.

Cara.

Darian's mind clung to the tiny scrap of information. He knew her name.

The dress slid up over her heart shaped ass.

Darian couldn't help it. He couldn't hold the shape of his wolf when the man in him was reacting so physically to Cara. He backed up a few feet as he began to shift back into a human. Darian didn't want her to stop, he didn't want the sounds of his bones shifting to disturb her. The white fur of his wolf shed away from his skin as his bones shifted back to their human position.

He couldn't stop watching her.

The curve of her lower back was every bit as sensual as the rest of her. Darian gulped as the gown was pulled free from her body. The twin curves of the sides of her fair breasts were all he could see from his angle behind her.

He wanted to see more but he held himself still. Already his shaft was hard and pulsing. Darian's human side was merely reacting to her physical body. He would not stoop so low as to mate with a murderer. He might share a body with the soul of a wolf but Darian was a man and he wasn't going to allow his body or his wolf to make his mind up for him.

She balled the gown up and tossed it onto the shore without looking in his direction.

Darian found himself wishing she would turn toward him and bare her naked beauty to him.

Ridiculous.

It wasn't as though Cara was the first naked woman he'd ever seen. Many of his pack were women, he'd seen them all shift. Their nudity was natural. Somehow, this was different.

Cara dipped under the surface, bending her knees. She'd only gone waist deep into the water before she began dipping her body under.

As she rubbed her skin vigorously with her hands and continued to rinse away the filth, Darian straightened with a start. The scent that filled the air, it was the same that woke him from his sleep. It was the same sweet, alluring smell that pulled him from the comfort of his bed and into action.

Darian swallowed hard watching her in disbelief.

He'd heard of fated bonding, but he'd never seen it in his lifetime. This scent, it was as described by the elders of his pack. If a wolf found his predestined mate, his wolf would immediately form an unbreakable bond. They belonged to each other from that day forward.

Cara is my predestined mate?

His wolf confirmed it with a protective growl.

She turned around at the sound. Her wounded arm covered the peaks of her breasts from his view, and her left hand held the blade pointed at him. Her eyes were like steel as she met his gaze.

Look at her, she's fierce, she's strong, and she's a warrior. She's perfect.

CHAPTER 5

The wolf was gone. In his place a young man stood. He was nearly naked with torn pants or shorts hanging loosely around his waist. His golden yellow eyes reminded Cara of the orange flames in a fire. His black hair slightly on the long side fell across his forehead and over part of his left eye. His gaze was intent on her. Everywhere his eyes roamed felt like a heated caress over her cold skin.

Cara recognized desire in his features. She stiffened. The filth from the water was so rank it was making her feel nauseous, and Cara knew the wound from the wolf bite was getting infected. She'd had no choice but to wash.

Naked in front of a shifter. Not smart, Cara.

She'd be lucky if all he did was force himself on her. Surviving an attack by a shifter had to be nearly impossible. The strength wielded by the creature would break her like toast.

She took a few steps back toward the shore. If she could get her dress on maybe the shifter would be put off by the smell. Maybe he would stop looking at her like she was something to eat.

The ground below the water's surface was slippery. Each step she took, Cara had to take slowly and carefully. As the water grew shallow, she could see his nostrils flaring. His eyes were on her waist. If she took another step he'd see more than she was willing to show.

"Stop. Staring. At. Me," she enunciated each word in a commanding tone. "Get out of here," she yelled. Cara hoped raising her voice would scare him off.

It didn't.

"You have nothing to fear from me," the shifter said. His voice was low, and heated.

"You can talk? I didn't know you had human intelligence."

His yellow eyes narrowed on her face. At least he was no longer trying to see her nakedness. "You know nothing of shifters."

"I know enough," Cara said. She let the bitterness she felt fill her voice. "You attacked me, and bit me. You're refusing to give me privacy. You're an animal, and as soon as I turn my back on you, I'm sure you'll try again to kill me."

The shifter lifted his lean, muscular arm as he pushed his hair from his eyes. The long red cut over his bicep was the cut she'd given him. "I should not have bitten you. I didn't know who you were."

"You still don't know who I am." A wave of dizziness washed over Cara and she fought to stay upright on the slippery rocks.

"You are, my Cara."

My Cara?

She gripped the blade harder, doing her best not to drop it. Her energy was seeping away. Cara knew she'd lost some blood from the bite but not so much she should be so weak.

"Cara, you're growing pale. Come out of the water. I swear, I won't hurt you."

"Stop looking at me. Then I'll come out," Cara growled at him.

To her surprise, the shifter turned around giving her his back. He'd actually listened to her.

It's just a trick. He's still going to try and kill me. I'm not stupid. I'm not going to fall for his trap.

Cara marched forward keeping her eyes on the defined, muscular back of the shifter. When she looked down to locate her night gown she spotted dozens of slimy black patches of mud all over her legs.

She went to swipe one off and the slippery fat thing moved under her fingers. Cara gasped as she realized her legs were covered in a slug like creatures.

"Don't pull it off. The head of the leech will detach and burrow into your skin. It will continue to suck your blood," the shifter told her.

"Suck my blood?" Cara felt another wave of dizziness. "How do I get them off?"

He went to the pouch the guard gave her and came back with flint and a candle. "Aldrich can't trade for a lighter?"

"What are you going to do with that?"

"Burn them. The heat will make them let go of you."

Cara sank to her knees. She was too light headed to stand. Too sick to her stomach to think. He lit the candle and applied the flame to the leach. The fat, black, slug-like thing fell off, dropping like a stone. A dozen tiny bleeding pin pricks marked her skin where the leech was feasting on her.

Tiny little bastard.

The shifter moved the flame to the next leech. The heat began to hurt but she refused to let the shifter see her pain. As soon as he saw weakness he would prey on it. That was what men like Aldrich, her father, and this shifter were like. They were the kind to prey on the weakness of others.

Knowing the things on her were sucking her blood made her want to cry, but she wouldn't cry in front of him. Cara wasn't sure why he was helping her at all.

He probably needs me alive to torture information out of me.

The shifter moved fast, going from one leech to the next. As the flame was applied higher, and higher on her legs the skin became more sensitive. The skin on the inside of her thigh hurt so much she couldn't keep her eyes from watering. Her mouth was clamped shut to hold in the cry of pain she refused to let out.

"I'm sorry it hurts," the shifter said as he gently lifted her leg to check the back of her thigh for any more. "Can you stand?"

Cara nodded even though she didn't know if she could. She wasn't about to tell the wolf she was so weak she couldn't stand.

His hands wrapped around her waist and he lifted her easily setting her on her feet. He moved around to her back, working quickly to remove the rest.

"Finished."

Cara heard him blow out the candle. She let out the breath she was holding, hating that it sounded like a whimper. The shifter swept her up in his arms. "Do you want to return to Aldrich Town for medicine?"

"No." Cara fought to get free of his hold.

He stopped walking and turned in a different direction. "Then you will come to my home. You need medicine."

"Put me down, creature," she demanded.

The muscle in his jawline flexed and he looked down at her as he continued walking. "I am Darian. I recommend you don't call any shifter a creature."

Cara, crossed her arms over her chest. "I need my dress. Please, just let me go. I don't know anything about Aldrich Town that would be of any use to you. I need to keep moving."

"Your dress is infested with disease and is septic. Why did you swim in that water? Was the man you killed attacking you?" He sounded hopeful.

Blood-thirsty creature.

"I fell in. The man who died, he saved my life." The shifter was looking at her again. Cara tried again to cover herself. "I demand to have clothes."

"I will provide you with all of your needs. You may rely on me. It seems destiny has plans for us. Though I can't say I understand them at the moment."

He was moving fast. Too fast. A wave of nausea crashed through her stomach again. Her brow was sweaty, her palms clammy. "I'm going to be sick," she tried to warn him but he didn't slow down. Turning her head toward the ground she threw up.

Her body was determined to expel the poison from the dirty water. Cara's entire body strained as she threw up again, and again.

"Your simple system can't fight the germs on its own. You need strong medicine. Cover your eyes and I will take you to my home where there is medical help."

If I cover my eyes he'll probably kill me. Stab me with my own blade or something. Oh no, where is my blade?

"I don't trust you. Please, just put me down."

"Why not? I'm trying to help you."

Cara shook her head. "You attacked me. You want to kill me."

"I was wrong. I thought you were a hunter."

"You want me to trust you? Put me down, Darian."

He stopped walking and set her on her feet with a huff of hot breath blasting through her wet hair. "Thank you…" Her vision swallowed up in darkness and she felt herself begin to fall.

Strong arms wrapped around her, catching her. "It's okay. I've got you, Cara. Stubborn, human." His lips, pressed against her temple, was the last thing she registered before she passed out.

CHAPTER 6

Cara lay limp in his arms. Her fever rose as her body tried to burn away the impurities from the dirty water. Cradling her close he kissed her temple again, wanting so much to taste her lips. The bond he had with her had to be the reason for his sudden desire to kiss and taste a human.

He wouldn't.

Darian promised Cara that he would take care of her, and he meant what he'd said. He used his vast speed to race through the forest.

Darian couldn't move as fast in his human form as he did when he was in his wolf shape, but it was close. He carried her up the incline to the Rizer pack community.

"Killian," Darian called out for their healer. "She's sick, and injured too," Darian said as he lay her gently on his bed.

Killian entered the room. His chiseled jaw line tight, no doubt because of the human on Darian's bed. Killian inclined his head to show proper respect, his curly dark brown hair falling forward as he did. He did not refuse to help as Darian knew he wouldn't. Killian with his wide shoulders and gruff exterior had a good heart.

Darian admired long, lean, exquisite body. He knew she would be punching him or trying to claw his eyes out if she were awake. Scolding himself for his invasion of her privacy he draped a blanket over her body.

Killian pushed his hand through his hair with a growl. "You bit her?"

"I thought she was a hunter," Darian snapped.

Killian looked up from Cara at Darian. "Is she a hunter?"

"No."

"How can you be certain?" Killian asked, frowning at Darian, his dark blue eyes shrinking under his dark scowling brows. "She could lead others here."

Darian smoothed the wet hair from her face, tucking it behind her ear. "Cara is unconscious. She doesn't know how to get here."

"She has fever, and signs of blood poisoning." Killian gestured to the purple veins beneath her pale skin.

Darian grimaced at the sight of his bite on her arm. "Cara fell in the septic water surrounding Aldrich's town. I think she may have swallowed some too."

Killian's frown deepened. "I will try to help her. Human medicine isn't the same as ours. She may not be strong enough to survive our methods."

"Cara is strong enough. She can't die, Killian," Darian told to his friend. "She... She is... mine."

Killian's brown eyes rounded at Darian. His jaw loosened and his mouth fell open. "You believe she is *fated* for you?"

Darian didn't know if that was true, he just knew that he was fated to Cara. She may not ever feel the same about him. The way she looked at him when she saw him was obvious that she despised shifters.

"I will do all that I can," Killian promised when Darian struggled for words to explain. He raced away to get whatever medical supplies he needed, leaving Darian to look at his mate.

Her arms were so thin and fragile, but he'd seen her strength. He'd seen her determination. She would live through this. Cara would heal and somehow, he would find a way to win her forgiveness.

"I will make this right, Cara. I promise."

Killian returned with two packs full of supplies. "Jules is worried about you," Killian said without meeting Darian's gaze. Jules was a determined she-shifter who made no secret of wanting to mate with Darian. He'd flirted with the idea. They'd shared a few kisses but he'd known even before he'd met Cara, that Jules would never be his mate.

He had to think of the pack.

Jules was too quick to react. She didn't consider the outcome of her actions or the effect it would have on the pack. Jules loved attention and she craved power. The youngest of her siblings, Jules had grown accustomed to getting what she wanted.

"My place is here with Cara," Darian said.

"Alpha, forgive me but if you want this human to survive after she is well enough to leave this room you must address the pack. You must prepare them for her presence here in our community. She still smells of Aldrich Town. Our pack will react on instinct." Killian began to dress the wound on her arm. His own struggle to accept her presence apparent in the set of his tight jaw.

Killian still suffered nightmares from the day their former alpha, Valor was murdered. Darian knew that Killian still blamed himself for bringing the injured man into their community. Many of the shifters even outside the Rizer wolf pack didn't trust humans. The warring and constant shift in alliances made relying on or trusting in a human, very dangerous.

Many opposed Killian when he saved the man who he found nearly dead on the edge of the mountain. Valor, however, praised Killian for showing mercy. He said that the pack should see his willingness to help the human as a sign of respect, as life in any form is a gift.

Killian swore to be responsible for the human. Valor made the decision to allow the man to stay while he needed medical treatment. After a week, the man awoke from his coma. Killian wanted to take him to the town that was settled beyond the forest at the base of the mountain.

It was Valor who insisted the man stay until he was well enough to return under his own power. Valor took an interest in the man who said he'd escaped from the latest siege by the bear shifters on Los Angeles. Valor wanted to know what the latest happenings were in the bigger city before the siege.

He also wanted to know how the man traveled so far north, he was after all just a human. The man told amazing tales of how he survived one desperate situation to the next. He continued to heal and Valor prolonged his stay.

While the pack left for the morning run one day, the man who'd fully recovered betrayed the pack and murdered the alpha.

The pack knew as Darian did, that it was Valor who chose to keep the human man so close. Killian was not responsible. Convincing the stubborn wolf of this proved impossible.

The whole community was fooled by him, not just Killian. If Killian was at fault, then they were all at fault.

"Are you well enough to care for her correctly?" Darian asked Killian offering him a way out if it proved to be too much to heal Cara.

Killian nodded as he continued to work. "Yes, Alpha. I will not allow her to die. This I vow." Giving his alpha a vow, Killian tied his destiny with Cara's outcome. If she died, it would be the alpha's right to take Killian's life as well.

Darian closed his eyes concentrating on feeling of magnetism he had with Cara. It was going to be difficult to leave the room. Killian was correct about the pack. They would have to be told. Cara's safety had to come before his desires, before his own, and even before that of the pack.

The urge to kiss her goodbye was nearly overwhelming. It was still too strange even to Darian to be drawn to the human. Kissing her in front of Killian proved to be too much and yet he couldn't quite leave without saying something to her. "Come back to me, Cara."

Darian could feel Jules' presence in the doorway before he straightened away from his destined mate. "If she wakes while I am gone, tell her I will be right back. Assure her that she is safe."

Killian inclined his head of dark curly hair. "I will."

Darian left his room and closed the door to keep others from disturbing Killian as he worked. Jules remained a step behind him. Her energy was wild even though she tried contain it. He could feel it snapping in the air around them like static.

"Why are we saving the human? She is of Aldrich town."

"I will explain to the pack. You will wait until then," Darian commanded using the authority in his voice that she would not dare disobey.

The energy in the air increased. Darian could feel her anger, jealousy, and fear. Normally he would try to soothe her, Jules being a member of his pack, but Darian couldn't. His thoughts were wrapped around Cara.

Seeing her turn toward him with the silver blade, ready to fight a fight she had no prayer of winning... It was the most beautiful, and the sexiest thing he'd ever seen. He clung to the memory. If she died, it would be all he had of her, and he would never take another.

"Shall I call the pack for you?" Jules asked him.

"This is a serious matter. I will call them." Darian looked at her, gauging to see if she was going to remain in control of herself, and of her wolf. Her short black hair framed her face, and her wild green eyes met my gaze. There was pain there. Rejection.

Jules was a proud woman. She would only grow angrier if Darian tried to soothe her or explain that he hadn't chosen to feel the way he did.

Darian decided to leave her alone for the time being, she would come to terms with Cara. She wouldn't have a choice. Neither did Darian, for that matter.

He howled, summoning the pack. He did not have long to wait. His pack was quick to come to his call.

Darian stood in the center of the courtyard looking his pack over as they arrived. The Rizer pack was larger than any of the other wolf shifter packs. It marked them as a formidable force among the shifter communities.

After Valor died Darian stepped up into the role of Alpha. He'd fought Rafi Le Roche for the position. It was brutal fight, but necessary. Everyone knew that Rafi still wanted the position of Alpha. For now though, he a played the part of submitting Rizer pack member.

Rafi also hated humans.

He was born of werewolves. It was a pure blood kind of superiority with Rafi. Darian too was born of werewolves, but his parents did not encourage hate. They were like Valor. They tried to teach Darian to be an accepting man.

Rafi's intolerance of humans renewed when the human killed Valor. He took pleasure killing the human hunters, forgetting the value of life.

The pack was nearly thirty shifters large. As Darian looked out at them not at all sure how he would tell them that he'd bonded with a human woman.

It was likely Rafi would take the opportunity to fight Darian again for the title of Alpha. Darian couldn't help the disappointment he felt toward Rafi. Hating humans like he did was not how Valor taught them to behave.

Swallowing, Darian knew he was guilty of this too. Hadn't he been ready to kill Cara before she'd lifted a finger against him?

"I know you can sense the stranger here," Darian began. "I brought her here after I attacked her."

"Why?" Jules asked shaking her head at him. "Why didn't you just finish her?"

Darian cut his eyes to Jules. She took a small step back and lowered her gaze.

"We suffered a great loss when Aldrich killed Valor. He betrayed our trust, and he darkened our hearts with hate."

Rafi's ears perked as he tilted his head to the right, his long black hair contrasting with his pale skin. His thick brows drew together at the bridge of his nose.

"I assumed so much about her when I saw her," Darian continued. He wanted to make them understand. He wanted them to recognize how wrong they were. "I saw a person dragging a dead body from the poisonous stale water. The body was bloodied, the neck broken."

"She killed him," Balder said folding his arms.

"It's what I thought too. I watched her, thinking she was pulling her victim from the water. I saw her cry for him and still I believed she killed him. She didn't. Aldrich killed him. The dead man saved Cara."

Rafi rolled his thick shoulders. His impatience palpable. "What does this human business have to do with us?"

"I watched Cara, attacked her. She fought me off and still I stalked after her biding my time. Injured and poisoned from the mote, she walked without resting to Everclear."

Ian, and Errol, the twins, widened their eyes, acknowledging that she was strong. They were the first to show any sign of accepting her.

"She bathed away the filth of the poison water and it was then that I caught her true scent." Darian hardened his gaze as he looked over his pack. "She is my mate. Any who cannot swear to protect her are not welcome to remain with the Rizer pack."

The collected intake of breath was followed by silence. Several moments passed with strained, unspoken words.

Ian bowed his head showing his allegiance to pack Rizer. Lena was next, her dark braids swung as she too bowed her head. Next, Errol. Then Maddock. The remaining pack members bowed their heads. All except for Rafi.

Rafi open and closed his hands at his sides. He was struggling with it, they could all see it. He looked up at Darian.

This is it.

"Do you mean to turn her? Do you truly believe her to be strong enough to be the female alpha to our pack?" Rafi asked.

Darian didn't expect Rafi to ask this question. However, refused to play games and tell Rafi anything other than the truth. "I bit her when I attacked. If she survives, she is already turned." Darian raised his voice, his tone demanding silence as he continued. "She's my fated partner. You know as well as I do, there is no choice in the matter when it comes to destined matches."

"What if you're wrong? We haven't seen a destined match in our lifetime. How do you know you're not mistaking?" Jules demanded her green eyes suspiciously moist. "What if she leaves? How will you lead us when this human from town Aldrich tears your insides to mush?"

Darian met her angry gaze. "If that is what will be, then another will have to challenge me for the position of alpha."

Jules grabbed Darian's arm. "Sever the tie now, while it's still new. Let her die. She is human. She is of town Aldrich, a sworn enemy of our pack. *Cara*, as you call her, is only here to tear the pack apart. Aldrich wants us weak. He sent her here. This is *his* doing."

His first instinct was to pull away from Jules. She was so jealous she could hardly contain it. Jules would say anything to cast doubt onto Cara even though she'd never met her.

The pack would not trust him to lead if he reacted on emotion alone. Darian removed her hand from his arm. "Cara is innocent. She is not Aldrich. She is *my mate*." Darian bit out the last two words. His voice echoed off the walls of the now quiet room.

Jules glared down at her feet, but made no move to leave.

At last Rafi took a step forward. "I will honor your wishes. You are my alpha."

Darian narrowed his gaze on the other wolf, surprised by his sudden wiliness to accept the outsider. The energy in the air quieted to a raw submission of his command.

It wasn't easy for them, nor was it easy for Darian.

There is peace among us. For now, at least

CHAPTER 7

Cara knew she was dreaming. She had to be. Darian, the shifter was smiling at her with a look of affection, and kindness. Cara knew better. Darian attacked her, he didn't care for her. The shifter wanted her dead.

It's too bad he has to be so handsome.

His wide frame and square shoulders were powerful. Darian's muscular chest and arms made him appear the perfect protector. His skin bore a warm healthy glow.

How nice for him that he gets to enjoy the sunshine while everyone inside the walls is confined to live in shadow.

His smile vanished when he noticed her looking at him. "Are you in pain?" Darian asked.

The baritone quality of his voice pulled her away from her negative musings. It was a masculine sound, yet smooth and rich. Cara watched him. He looked uncomfortable, uncertain. "I'm glad," his eyes dipped lower to her chest and then back to her face. "you're awake."

A heated shiver ran down her spine and was unlike anything she'd ever felt before. "I'm not awake. This is a dream," she told him.

"Is it? How do you know?"

Cara smiled at him, drinking in the beauty of his wild, golden eyes.

"I'm warm and the bed is soft." His interested gaze shifted to the floor. Again, he appeared uncomfortable. "Besides, if I were awake, I would be married to Aldrich."

Darian straightened, a dark scowl on his face. "You are engaged to Aldrich? You love him? Has he... touched you, Cara?"

There is a lot of talking in this dream.

"I don't want to talk about Aldrich. Don't I even get to escape him in my dreams?"

A ghost of a smile touched Darian's lips. "You do not care for Aldrich?"

"I hate him."

He nodded, his shoulders relaxing momentarily before he was back to scowling. "Did he hurt you?"

Cara rolled onto her back and squinted as the rays of sun warmed her face. It felt so nice and yet so bright. The sun never hit directly into any of the windows in her home. The wall cast too great a shadow on all sides.

"Is he the one who did this?" Darian asked, his finger gently ran over the skin on the side of her face. It was still tender.

I shouldn't be able to feel pain if I'm dreaming. Right?

Cara tried to sit up, but pain ripped down her arm. She gritted her teeth and closed her eyes, refusing to cry out or shed a tear in front of the shifter.

"Cara, you don't know how much I regret hurting you."

She glared up at him, her lips pressed tightly together.

"I don't blame you for being angry. I thought you were a hunter. One of Aldrich's hunters."

Cara used her left hand to sit up and then caught the blanket as she realized she wasn't wearing anything. No wonder he'd been looking her over. Cara hugged the blanket over her chest. She was too angry to shrink away even if she was horrified at being naked and alone with him.

"You can't let the people of Aldrich Town eat? If we dare come out to try and catch food, you just have to kill us?"

"No, Cara," Darian said, her name on his lips sounding like an endearment.

"It's because of you that we've all been caged in by the wall. We are all at the mercy of Aldrich. You showed up, and nearly overnight, Havenhurst became Aldrich Town."

Darian frowned at her as if he didn't know this information. He had to know. He was older than she was and she remembered the wall going up.

"The wall protects us against you and *your kind*," Cara said letting anger fill her words. "You took away the sun. Do you realize that?"

"Your people were never the target of the Rizer wolf pack."

Cara barked out a laugh. "Is that why the Miller family no longer has any children? Shifters killed both of their sons soon after you and the other shifters settled here. They were just kids. What harm could they have done to you?"

Darian scowled at her. "Are you accusing my pack of killing children?" He stood up leaning over the bed.

Cara shielded her eyes, thinking he would be in the torn-up shorts but he was wearing black pants that rode low on his hips. The V shape of muscle and a light dusting of black hair disappeared under the waist of the pants.

"The Rizer pack doesn't kill innocent children. We only kill the hunters. Hunters who have killed members of my pack." His voice held a power to it that she didn't understand. She didn't like him or anyone else having power over her.

She fought the pull to lower her gaze and accept what he said as the truth. Instead, Cara stood up, facing him. "We're starving inside the wall. The hunters probably killed a wolf because they were hungry enough to eat anything."

Darian met her gaze with a measured look of his own. "Careful how you speak of my pack, Cara. They are my *family*, not food."

Cara was ready to defy him but he didn't raise his voice to her when he asked her to be careful. He didn't act as though he would hit her.

He will. They all do.

"Your *family* kills our hunters and leaves the rest of us dependent upon a man whose cruelty is unlike anything you could possibly imagine."

"You're wrong Cara. We've seen what Aldrich is capable of, first hand. Aldrich promises your hunters wealth in exchange for my family's wolf skin. I've lost five from my pack, and that doesn't include Valor."

Cara frowned. "If you hate being hunted by Aldrich, why don't you leave? Take your family and go."

"Aldrich has to be stopped," Darian answered. He reached out lightly grazing the tender skin on the side of her head, his eyes hardened. "Who did this to you? Aldrich?"

Cara swiped at his hand. He caught her wrist firmly. "What do you care? My arm hurts a lot worse." Cara held up her bandaged wrist and forearm as a reminder of his bite.

Darian nodded. "I imagine it does. All I can do is promise you that I will never hurt you again. None of my pack will harm you. We will protect you."

Cara didn't trust the warmth she felt at his words. She didn't trust the feeling of relief that eased the tension in her back. "You said that Aldrich has to be stopped. Stopped from doing what, exactly?"

"If I tell you, Cara, I want something from you in return."

The heat from his hand on her wrist felt strange to her. She twisted free. "What?" Cara asked hugging the blanket tighter around her body.

Darian's gaze returned to the bruise on her face.

"That's all?" Cara asked him. "You want to know who hit me?"

The shifter inclined his head.

"You go first," Cara said.

He exhaled quietly, his golden eyes lowered to the blanket covering her legs. "Valor purchased two hundred acres of land for our community, just outside your little town. He wanted our pack to have the room we need, and the wild life our wolves demand. It is in the wolf's nature to hunt. An injured man came to our pack from the city."

"Aldrich?" Cara asked.

"Unfortunately, yes."

Cara stiffened as Darian edged closer to her.

What does he want from me? He could have killed me a dozen times by now.

"Aldrich convinced our Alpha, Valor, that he wanted to learn about our ways. Teach humans about us so that they could learn not to fear us." His fingers trailed over her naked back. The sensation warm and electric.

"What are you doing?" Cara asked him. Fear making her voice hike up in pitch.

Darian pressed his warm palm against her back. "I want you to become accustomed to my touch."

Cara gave him a warning glare.

"If you ask me to stop, I will stop. Cara, I promised you already that I will never hurt you. I will not force you to do anything you don't want to do." He hesitated. "I don't want you to fear me."

His hand was still on her back. The sensation it gave her was too confusing to understand.

"Valor allowed Aldrich to live in our community for several months. He won the trust of the pack. We all were taken in by his trickery."

"What happened?" Cara asked trying to tolerate his hand against her skin. She still didn't understand why it was important to Darian what she thought of him.

Darian's hand began to rub her back in a slow circular motion. The intimacy of the touch proved to be more than she was comfortable receiving. Cara side stepped away from his hand, breaking the physical connection.

The shifter's hand fell down at his side. "He asked Valor to make him one of the pack, a shifter."

"He's one of you?" Cara remembered the way he'd bitten the guard and the blood that ran down his face. It was terrifying.

"No," Darian said. "Valor refused him. Aldrich took his knowledge of our kind and used it against Valor. Aldrich murdered Valor by stabbing him in the back with a silver blade. Then he drank from Valor in hopes of changing himself into a shapeshifter."

Cara couldn't help it, she had to look at Darian as he spoke. She had to see his golden eyes because his words were full of emotion, a trait that she'd always been taught shifters didn't have. When Cara's father first started apologizing for hitting her she believed him that he was sorry.

Later she learned that she could see if he was sincere by looking into his eyes. The truth was always there in his gaze.

Darian's eyes were so much more complex than her father's. She could see sorrow, anger, and Compassion in his golden depths. "Why would he do that? It doesn't make sense."

"The bite of a werewolf infects the blood of a human. It changes them into a shapeshifter. Aldrich knew the shapeshifter mutation is in the blood. We believe this was the reason he drank Valor's blood. He was trying to change his own." Darian was watching her closely.

"Did it work?"

"It changed his blood if that's what you mean, but he is not a werewolf. He is more like a rabid human. Aldrich craves blood, violence, and power. The werewolf blood he drank from Valor gave him great strength. However, not so great he can survive a fight with the pack."

Cara felt his gaze on her mouth. She ran her tongue over her suddenly dry lips. "Why not destroy the wall and get him?"

"He knows our weaknesses. Aldrich was the one who killed the children and scared your people into building the wall. A wall laced with elements that are poisonous to our kind. The water you climbed out of that surrounds the wall, it too is poisonous to us."

Cara took another step back from Darian, as she thought of Aldrich. He was like a wild animal, but Darian actually was half wolf. His promises were worthless.

"And Aldrich never leaves the town," Cara finished for him. "So, you're waiting out here, and he sends desperate men to come and hunt your kind down."

Darian looked at the space she'd created between them. "I'd never thought of the hunters like that. They come at us armed with silver, and we can't just allow them to kill us."

Cara didn't respond because she didn't know what to say. He was right about that, but since his kind were so much bigger and stronger, she felt they should do something to stop the hunters. Couldn't they stop them, and spare them?

"Your turn," Darian said.

"My turn?" Cara arched a brow.

Darian gestured to her cheek. "The bruise on you face."

"Oh. My father hit me," Cara answered she didn't know why he was so determined to know.

"Your father hit you, and was going to allow you to be taken by Aldrich?"

Cara shrugged. "You haven't been trapped in a cage for years at a time. You couldn't possibly understand the kind of pressure my father is under." Darian didn't look the least bit convinced. "Aldrich would have starved my father to death if he refused him."

Darian closed the space between them so fast that she didn't even see him move. He framed her face with his hands not allowing her to back away. "I would starve to death if it meant saving you from Aldrich. I would fight an army to keep you safe, Cara." The look in his golden yellow eyes was full of sincerity and something else.

Lust? Like Aldrich?

"You want to have sex. That's why you're being nice to me?"

Darian exhaled releasing her face from his hands. "No, Cara. I don't want to have sex with you. I don't want to care about you. I don't want to be tied to you. I don't like feeling protective of you or sorry for your horrible circumstances."

"I never asked you to feel sorry for me."

"It doesn't matter what I want. It only matters what is and will be."

He wasn't making any sense. "If you don't want to have sex then why do you keep touching me and trying to get me to become accustomed to you?"

"You're a part of my pack now."

Cara's eyes widened as her heart seemed to trip mid rhythm and stumble into a run within her chest. "Because you bit me?"

"Yes."

That must be why it feels so funny when he touches me. It must be why I want to accept everything he says as the truth.

Cara turned away from him and walked over to the open window. Fresh air blew her hair up and off her neck. Not even a hint of the mote staining the air. It was clean and fresh.

I should be furious. Shouldn't I?

She leaned on the windowsill.

If I'm a shifter I can protect myself from Aldrich, from my father. I can fight Darian when he attempts to control me.

A smile curved Cara's lips and she shut her eyes enjoying the feel of the wind on her face. "What does being a member of your pack require of me?"

"Require of you?"

Cara looked over her shoulder at him. "Yes. Do I have to kill the people who come out of Aldrich Town?"

"You won't be a wolf for several weeks yet. It usually takes at least a month before your first shift. You will be required to support the pack. Defend the pack as you would a family, because now they are your family."

Darian watched Cara, waiting for her to freak out. To explode in anger. She hated shifters only this morning. Where was all that hatred now?

"You are not upset?"

"Upset?" Cara asked, the smile on her face the first genuine joyful expression Darian saw on her face. "I should thank you. You've given me just what I need so that I can take care of myself."

"You're not alone anymore. The pack is your family and we will protect you."

I don't need their protection.

"The hunters will kill you if you venture outside of Rizer land without the pack. As you say, they are desperate."

"Not if I walk up to them before I turn, right?"

Darian's fisted his hands at his sides. "Do you wish to return to Aldrich Town?"

When she didn't answer, Darian frowned at her. "I command you not to leave Rizer land without a member of the Rizer pack."

Her spine stiffened. She was feeling the power of the alpha. Just like that Darian had snatched away the freedom he'd just given her. She glared at him with as that trapped, claustrophobic sensation returned. "You're forcing me to stay here?"

"I am protecting you."

She narrowed her sharp gaze further. "That's what they said when they built the wall."

CHAPTER 8

"You seem less than happy," Killian stated as Darian stomped down the hallway, away from his chamber leaving Cara behind. "She does not wish to marry? Surely the fated bonding will begin to take hold with her soon. She's a shifter now, even if she has yet to shift."

Darian eyed his friend. "I didn't tell her that we're destined."

"Why not? You seemed quite certain before."

"I am certain," Darian growled. He looked up and down the hallway for prying ears. "Just because I feel protective of her, attracted to her physically doesn't mean I'm ready to pair myself with her just yet."

Killian chuckled. "Too late for that, Darian. You've already announced to the pack she's to be your mate. You need to make it official."

"I won't command her to have me. Trust me, she would hate me if I commanded her to submit."

"Like she hates you for commanding her to stay on Rizer pack land?"

Darian stopped walking. "You were listening?"

"I was returning to be sure she was healing. I did not intend to intrude. Now that I have," Killian continued. "She doesn't seem the type at all who will be suited to the life of a Rizer pack member."

"You've already said it's too late to back out of it. You're wrong anyway, Killian. She's not suited to be a beta. Cara is meant to be the female alpha to my male alpha."

Killian's lips pressed together and he inclined his head. "Where are you going?"

"For a run. Watch after Cara. See that she doesn't get herself in too much trouble. I won't be long."

* * *

THE WHITE WOLF that streaked across the stretch of green land, had to be Darian. Cara was quite certain she recognized him as the same wolf that bit her arm.

I've got to get out of here. No way in hell am I allowing myself to be trapped inside another cage.

Cara went over to the closet. True to the traits of his gender she found most of the clothing piled up on the floor. There were a few shirts hanging in the closet. She ran her hand over the thick material in awe of the quality.

The green shirt would probably serve as the best camouflage. She removed the shirt from the hanger and slipped it on over her head. It hung low on her, almost to her knees. Cara opened up drawers and found torn shorts with elastic waistbands.

Sifting through the pile of them she found a pair that would be long enough to offer her a bit of warmth. Once she had them on she went to the closed door and listened.

Nothing. Maybe they are all sleeping?

She turned the knob and pulled the door inward, peeking out into the hallway she met the eyes of a man similar to Darian in coloring and in the look of distain Darian gave her in his wolf form.

Uneasiness knotted in her stomach. This shifter did not look as tolerant of her as Darian had and even he told her he didn't want her around. He was just stuck with her since he bit her.

Cara stood a bit straighter meeting his distant gaze. "Darian said that I'm part of the pack."

"I know." The man with dark curly black hair answered.

The tone of his voice left no mystery as to how he felt about her presence. *Good, so he won't stop me from leaving.*

Cara exited the room and turned left. It was the way she'd seen Darian go when he'd left the room.

"Where are you going?" The shifter asked.

A quick glance over her shoulder and Cara saw that he was following her. "Are you my prison guard or what?"

"This isn't a prison. It's our home."

"So, leave me alone and let me explore it," Cara snarled right back. She continued walking. The shifter waited until she was several yards away before he began following her again.

You are my prison guard, aren't you?

Cara jogged down the wide stair case and pushed open the double doors at the bottom. She thought she was outside and free to make a break for it but she was wrong. The double doors opened up into a large courtyard.

People were talking but as soon as she stepped out silence filled the courtyard. A woman reached down and snatched up a small child holding the toddler close as if saving him from Cara.

The man at her side began shifting. It was like a chain reaction. Once he started shifting so did the rest of the pack. Everyone except for Cara and the young children.

Cara was terrified but what could she do? Run? They'd just catch her and besides she already knew that predators liked to chase, catch and kill.

She remained still for several moments listening to the low growl emitting from the pack collectively.

"Remain still," the man with the dark curly black hair told her from behind her.

Cara spotted another door across the way.

I need to try that door and see if I can find an exit in this place.

Putting one foot in front of the other Cara started across the

AMELIA WILSON

courtyard. The steady growl grew louder the closer she came to the pair in the center of the courtyard.

"You don't like me, and I don't like you," Cara said. "Let me pass and I'll get out of here and leave you alone."

The black wolf with green eyes snarled. Its ears flattened as its black lips curled back, revealing sharp teeth. Cara looked past the black wolf at the doors.

Live in this cage or escape Cara. Pick one.

Cara continued forward as though the wolf wasn't blocking her path.

"Cara, stop," the guy at the double doors told her. "Jules is warning you to stop."

"She's not the alpha though, is she?" Cara said looking directly at the green eyes of the wolf.

A pair of yellow and white wolves walked in front of Cara blocking her path by Jules. These wolves were not behaving in the same aggressive manner.

Cara walked around them and continued to the door. There was only five more feet to cross and she'd make it to the doors.

Just as she neared the door a black and gray wolf circled into her path. The dark eyes of the wolf peered at her around the snarl and flash of teeth he was showing her.

"If you were going to hurt me you would have done it by now," Cara told him, but really, she was trying to reassure herself. The clap of his jaws made her jump inside. She managed to keep a calm exterior. Cara refused to back away.

The werewolves behind Cara began to shift back into their human forms.

"Rafi, stand down. She is not threatening you," A woman with long blond hair said.

The black and gray wolf didn't budge.

Cara thought she saw anger in the eyes of the wolf.

Darian will be back soon and I won't be able to escape.

She stepped forward. Rafi snapped at her ankles and despite her best efforts she stepped back.

The snarl that cracked through the air was like whip. Everyone behind her seemed to shrink back and away. Cara had an overwhelming need to bow low to the ground. She fought the urge but it was like fighting against gravity in a freefall. Cara fell onto her hands and knees as the white wolf of Darian attacked Rafi.

Powerful hands took hold of her and pulled her back and away from the battle. Cara couldn't take her eyes off of the two wolves rolling, and crashing into columns. She saw flashes of white teeth, around clash of black and white fur standing up on end.

Blood.

Red marked the ground where they continued to war.

"Stop it," Cara yelled at them but they didn't even slow.

"Stay back," the blond woman told Cara.

Cara took a small step back not sure what good it would do. "Why are they fighting?"

"Rafi threatened you. He snapped at you."

But, he didn't even touch me. I'm not even part of this pack.

The concrete cracked as Darian slammed Rafi onto the ground. It was a brutal sound, filled with pain, and unyielding power. The black wolf rolled onto his back with an anguished whimper.

Right away the white wolf began to shift. His golden eyes were on Cara, they were intense.

Cara knew he was angry. It was obvious she'd been trying to leave even after he'd told her, commanded her, not to do so. The white fur fell away from his skin evaporating as it fell to the earth. His bones moved under his skin in ripples and sharp points until he was standing in front of her.

His golden eyes ran over her from head to toe. The scowl on his face softening. "Are you hurt, Cara?"

Am I hurt?

"You're bleeding," Cara told him.

"Was she hurt, Killian?" Darian demanded of the shifter with the black curly hair.

Killian didn't say anything. He must have indicated to Darian that she wasn't hurt. Cara didn't know because she was too afraid to take her eyes off of Darian. Any moment he would strike her to the ground. It would hurt but she'd live through it now that she had shifter blood. Right?

"No one, threatens Cara," Darian's powerful voice echoed through the courtyard. He looked over his shoulder at Rafi who was still in the submissive position on his back.

Darian approached Killian, his golden eyes were blazing. "I told you to protect her."

"She is unharmed, Alpha," Killian answered, his eyes lowered. "She is the warrior you said she is, I did not interfere because Cara was earning the respect of the pack on her own."

I was?

Darian's frown remained in place. "When were you going to step in? After Rafi drew blood?"

Killian's dark blue eyes rose up to meet Darian's. "I believe Rafi was responding out of injured pride when Cara did not cower from him. If you had not interfered, I believe Cara would have won the stand-off."

"Cara, hasn't shifted. She doesn't have a prayer of fighting off Rafi."

"I fought *you*, off," Cara said before she could think better of it.

Darian looked at her, his annoyance with her clearly growing. "I held back."

That much was obvious from the fight she'd just witnessed. Cara lifted her chin anyway. "So was I."

"I'm sure you were," Darian said. His tone dismissive.

Cara's cheeks burned, her teeth clenched together.

The woman with the short black hair and green eyes, Jules, they called her when she was a wolf, was smiling at Cara's discomfort. Cara lowered her gaze turning over the fact in her mind that Jules was exhibiting the same bully mentality that Cara identified with men.

Suddenly, the realization that there was so much she didn't know about the world, about anyone or anything outside of Aldrich Town. The feeling was like a burning cold ooze swimming through her system.

Cara walked away from the pack meeting in the courtyard. She could feel Darian watching her. Cara didn't turn back to get permission or offer an explanation of where she was going.

The door she'd tried to take earlier led into an oversized room, Cara didn't stop to notice more than the high ceilings and large space she needed to cross. She found herself standing in a hallway and then another oversized room.

How do I get out of here?

"Darian asked me to escort you. Where do you want to go?" The blond shifter woman asked.

"Outside. I just want to get outside."

The woman nodded her head and led the way back down the hallway taking the opposite direction than the one Cara tried. She opened the double doors at the end of the hallway. Cool air rushed inside.

Cara followed the woman outside and continued walking even when the other woman stopped. Cara passed her and just kept on moving. She started to run up the incline. The mountain that she'd dreamt of climbing, she was on it.

I want to see the other side.

Tears rolled down her face. She swiped at them and kept climbing. The blond woman was following at a distance. Cara knew she wasn't getting away but if she accomplished one of her dreams, that would be something. Wouldn't it?

CHAPTER 9

Darian stood on the roof of the Rizer fortress.
He could see Cara climbing the mountain with the wind in her hair the cold stone under her feet and that same determined stiff spine he'd seen when she'd pushed herself in the forest.

"Will you follow her?" Killian asked.

"I haven't decided yet. Kate is following her."

Killian climbed out onto the roof. "I am sorry that you believe I wouldn't have interfered in time to keep Cara safe."

Darian exhaled. "I haven't ever felt this way about anyone Killian."

"Is it wonderful? To be in love?"

"No," Darian growled. "I don't know that I am in love. I'm protective of her, overly so, as you pointed out. I'm attracted to her even when I find myself displeased with her, I have an urge to kiss her. She hates me, and I don't know how to act around her."

Killian bowed his head. "I can't say that sounds like something I would want to be bothered with."

"She's so defensive."

"Like an injured wolf. She trusts no one," Killian mused.

Cara was coming to the top of the slope where the mountain shot up in a vertical climb.

At least she'll realize she has to stop and come back.

Darian and Killian were both quiet as they watched Cara reach the stop at the mountain wall. He waited for her to turn back. Maybe she would sit down and refuse to return.

Cara began to run her hands over the wall.

There's no way up Cara. You have to turn around.

The pack was watching her from below, Darian realized as they congregated outside. Now Cara would have to return to after a public failure.

She paced the flat wall back and forth like a caged animal giving him an undeniable visual of what Cara must have felt like inside that too-small, walled in town.

No wonder she reacted the way she did when I commanded her to stay inside the Rizer pack land. How can I make her understand that I'm trying to protect her?

"You may have to retrieve her," Killian said. "I don't think she's going to give up."

Darian waited watching Cara as she continued to try and find a way up the incline.

"Let her try until she's satisfied it can't be done."

Killian nodded.

Two hours passed during which Darian watched her cling to the flat wall and fall over and over again.

"I can't keep watching this," Darian said at last. "Enough is enough."

Killian shook his head. "You were right to wait. She has to be close to giving up."

"Are you blind? She's never going to give up."

"What will you do with a woman who will never give up trying to leave you?"

Darian leapt, beginning his descent from the roof to the ground, using the balconies and over hangs as his ladder. He continued watching the woman as he ran toward her. Her next fall would probably knock her out.

She'd already hit her head at least twice.

When he started up the final incline, Kate held her hand up to him. Darian followed her gaze to Cara. She was back in that same damn spot on the flat face of the wall. "She's going to fall again," Darian said.

"She worked hard to get where she is, allow her to finish her attempt."

Darian said nothing but continued up the incline. He would not interfere with Cara's attempt to climb but he'd be damned if he was going to watch her fall one more time.

Cara was staring at a spot well outside her reach. Her legs were pulled in close like a frog preparing to leap.

Shit, Cara.

He stood beneath Cara looking up at her limbs shaking with the strain.

"You're here to stop me?" Cara asked without looking at him.

"No, Cara. I'm here to catch you if you fall."

When she looked down at him his heart ached at the sight of her red eyes and wet face. "Why? I thought I wasn't allowed to leave."

"I was…" Darian looked back down the incline where Kate was still standing and would no doubt hear him. "I was wrong to command you to stay on Rizer land. You are free to come and go as you please."

"You're not going to trick me into staying," She said turning her face away from him again.

Darian laughed. He didn't know what else to do. "I don't have to trick you. I could just command you until you submit, but I'm not."

"I'm leaving."

"So, leave already," Darian growled.

Cara leapt.

Darian held his breath hoping for her despite himself that she'd make it, that her hands would stretch out far enough and catch hold.

Come on, Cara.

Her left hand slid over the smooth rock missing the grip.

Darian moved under her to catch her but her right hand found a hold. Cara's body smacked into the wall as she held on. The pack started howling in applause for her, though he wasn't sure if she understood that's what they were doing.

"Don't stop now," Darian called up. "You've got this, Cara."

She reached up with her left hand grabbing onto the same grip. Her legs clung to the wall and little by little she continued to climb. Darian leapt up and began climbing behind her.

With that mighty jump, Cara defeated the most difficult part of the climb. The rest went by relatively fast. When she reached the summit, she stopped to gaze down at the other side.

"Now what?" Darian asked as he came to stand beside her.

"I don't know," Cara admitted. "I thought when I got up here I'd see a new mountain to climb to, or a big city."

Darian nodded. His hands itching to take her in his arms and make her accept the comfort he wanted to give her.

Cara's blue eyes swept over the desolate landscape on the other side of the mountain. "I thought shifters were evil," Cara swallowed. "Today I watched you fight your own family to stand up for me. I don't know why you'd do that. I'm no one."

"He was wrong to threaten you," Darian said. He wasn't admitting to anything more when she was so close to leaving anyway.

"My own family has stood by when I've been handed worse than just threats." She cleared her throat. Darian could see she was fighting off tears. "I stood by too. I'm not any better than my father. When Aldrich took that young woman and we all knew she was being mistreated, we didn't help her." Cara didn't try anymore to hold back her tears. "I didn't help her."

Darian reached out and wiped away the tears running over her bruised cheek. "It looks like you stood up against Aldrich wherever you could."

Cara nodded. "I can't leave knowing there will be another girl taken, like the one he took last. I want to help you and your family stop him."

A common goal. Yes. I can work with that.

"Thank you."

CHAPTER 10

I'll catch you if you fall.

Cara remembered Darian's promise when he stood under her on the mountain. His words warmed her and embarrassed her at the same time as she thought on them.

The way I've been behaving was all based on what I thought I knew. I don't know anything.

They were on their way back down the mountain, the shifter Kate walking with them. Cara followed Darian glad to let him take the lead. It gave her the chance to think. For one thing, Cara realized she had to stop thinking of Darian and his pack as blood thirsty creatures.

It wasn't just that Darian showed her patience far beyond what was offered by her father. The fact was, Cara was bitten and infected with the mutation. She was a shifter and not only did she still feel emotion and have complex thoughts, she had her eyes opened as though even her mind was trapped in shadow before she'd left Aldrich town.

"I have a question," she said after accepting that she had a lot to learn.

"A question for me?" Darian asked not looking back in her direction.

Cara licked her lips realizing too late that she was going to come off sounding stupid with her basic questions. She glanced back at Kate and hoped the woman wouldn't think less of her.

When she looked forward again she ran right into Darian, who'd stopped walking and turned back when she didn't ask her question. His arms came around her immediately, steadying her with ease.

The warmth of Darian's arms around her, was comforting.

Is this what it's supposed to feel like to have family?

Looking up at him she tried to read in his expression if he felt anything unusual. His expression didn't tell her anything at all.

"You had a question?" He removed his arms from around her.

"Yes. I know it's going to be the first of many to come. I'm realizing there is a lot that I don't know."

Darian's golden eyes widened as he looked at her.

I've already said something wrong?

"Why are you looking at me like that? Did I say the wrong thing?"

"No," Darian answered. His eyes remained widened though as he turned and started walking again. Cara walked along-side him so she could see he still wore the surprised expression. "Ask your question."

Cara realized she was staring at him and averted her gaze from his masculine profile. "When I turn or shift, is it going to hurt?"

"Yes."

She exhaled, figuring it would but hoped she was wrong. "Will I have control over when I shift or how much I shift?"

"The first time will not be your choice. After that, you will learn to control when you shift."

"Will I be violent when I'm a wolf?"

"When you were bitten, and the mutation was added into your blood stream it didn't only change your abilities," Kate said. She patted Cara gently on the back.

More physical contact. Good but not the same feeling as the one I feel from Darian. I wonder why?

"Life is a gift, Cara. There are many souls waiting for the right to a body. The mutation gene opens your body up to accept an additional host."

"What?" Cara stopped walking. "You're saying another spirit will occupy my body? That isn't logical. I don't know if I believe in the existence of spirits at all."

Kate nodded. "I felt very similar when Valor tried to explain this to me."

"Will this spirit argue with me and take over my body?"

"It will be the spirit of your wolf. She will be a companion and friend. Her love for you will grow like your love for her."

Cara blew out a long breath. "I don't understand how I'll grow to love a wolf that wants to kill."

Darian half smiled. "Your spirit wolf is already with you, Cara. You haven't gone on a murdering rampage yet."

"I would notice if a wolf soul was in my body."

"She's there," Kate agreed with Darian. "If she wasn't, Darian's position as Alpha would mean nothing to you. His commands would leave you unaffected."

Cara frowned. "How will I know what feelings are mine and which are hers?"

"The pull and tug," Kate smiled. "When you feel have an urge to do something you know isn't from you, you'll know it's her. She'll emerge to protect you and the people you love. Your strong emotions are hers, and some of hers will become yours."

"Is my wolf in need of a lot of human contact?"

Kate shrugged. "I don't know what you mean?"

"Darian said he wanted to help me grow accustomed to his touch when I first arrived here. Is that for my wolf?"

Kate smiled a toothy grin as she looked at Darian. "I imagine that has more to do with you being his destined mate." She laughed and sprinted away.

Darian's ears were red and so was the back of his neck.

"Destined mate?"

* * *

DARIAN COULD FEEL Cara's eyes on him and knew that he had to try and explain it to her. She might be willing to stay and help kill Aldrich but that didn't have anything to do with caring about him or the Rizer pack.

When she started asking questions with an open mind, Darian thought he was dreaming. Never once did he meet a human, turning shifter or not, who was willing to admit they were clueless about the realities of life.

Her admission made him take a look at himself. Darian was humbled as he realized she was stronger in character than himself. She was angry with herself for not helping a woman in need, and she recognized openly that her knowledge was lacking. Darian didn't think once of the hunters he killed as victims. He saw them as extensions of Aldrich.

Cara accused him of stealing the sun from the people of Aldrich town. How could he not have considered citizens of the town as victims when he knew so well how manipulative Aldrich could be?

"You said before that you didn't want to feel all those different things you were feeling. Was that because of the destined mate thing?" Cara asked.

I wish I had not said those things to you.

"Yes." Darian stopped walking and faced Cara. "I meant what I said when I told you that I will never force you to do anything you don't want to do. I also meant it when I told you that you're free and that I won't force you to stay."

Cara nodded but didn't say anything.

"Do you want me to explain what Destined Mates, means?"

"No. I believe I understand." She started walking again.

She did not look afraid, happy, sad, it was as if he'd told her something as insignificant as his shoe size, and considering he didn't wear shoes, it was an extremely insignificant piece of information. Out of everything Cara learned over the past five hours, shouldn't learning that she was destined to be married to Darian rank high on the scale of priority questions?

Maybe she didn't think she could care for him and since he'd promised not to force her into anything she wasn't worried. Or perhaps, she felt something too?

Ridiculous. She would have said something if she was beginning to care for me.

Cara asked questions about training to fight so that she could be useful against Aldrich. Darian told her he would make sure she was trained even though he had no intension of allowing Cara anywhere near Aldrich.

Every time Darian saw the bruise on her face when he looked at her it made him want to find a way inside the wall to find Cara's father. The way she'd defended his abuse as a symptom of being enclosed in the town meant it was not a random incident. It was an ongoing practice of his and it was why Cara didn't understand what real love was.

If she did understand what it was, she didn't know how to accept it.

"I will train very hard. You won't have to protect me," Cara was saying.

"I believe you will. This won't change the fact that I will protect you."

Cara sped up her pace so that she was walking beside him. Her blue eyes were wide. "Darian, I know you had to step in with Rafi but that was because I haven't shifted yet. Once I have a sharp pair of teeth too it'll be a fair fight."

Darian smiled. He couldn't help but admire her warrior spirit shining through. "I can imagine. Rafi will be sorry he ever tried to stand in your path."

"He is already, isn't he? It wasn't any small lesson you taught him."

Darian only nodded. If she knew how strong his protective instinct was in those moments when he discovered Rafi growling at her she would consider him a violent man and Darian didn't want her to look at him and see any similarities to her father or Aldrich.

When they returned home, the pack welcomed her as they should have in the beginning. She'd won them over with her bravery and of course that insane leap she'd taken.

Determined to take things slow with Cara, Darian resisted the urges he had to touch her hand, or feel the texture of her short hair. He sat stoic at her side through dinner. When her leg brushed against his and his mind turned to showing her just how good it could feel to allow him to touch her, he kept it to himself.

After dinner most of the pack was in need of a run. Darian needed the exercise more than the rest of the pack. He knew that when he returned Cara would be sharing his room. It would be a long night of smelling her sweet scent and looking at a beautiful woman, who'd taught him more about himself in a few short hours than he'd learned in a lifetime before her.

"I will stay with her," Ian offered before Darian could ask. "We can all feel the energy you're putting out there, if you don't go run some of it off, all the mated members of the pack will be reproducing like its mating season."

"Thanks, Ian," Darian smiled. "Protect her."

"I will." Ian, his ice blue eyes solemn.

Darian slapped Ian's wide back muscular back and returned to Cara's side. Kate was telling Cara where to find the spare clothes kept for new members of the pack and as replacements. Darian waited until Kate finished before he spoke. "Ian is going to stay with you."

"Where are you going? Are you going after Aldrich?"

"No, not unless he dares to leave the protection of the wall. We will be running the perimeters to make sure there are no hunters looking to attack."

Cara nodded, lowering her gaze.

"I will give them every chance to run away," Darian promised ignoring the way the pack looked at him. He would explain to them what Cara taught him and knew they would understand.

"You will?" Her smile and the light in her blue eyes made him ache with the need to kiss her. Darian inclined his head, too afraid of what he might say if he spoke at the moment.

No doubt something ridiculous would spill out of his mouth in an attempt to win Cara's heart. There was nothing he could say that would change the fact that he stalked her and bit her.

Darian knew he had no right to even hope she would grow to love him as he was for her.

"Does your spirit wolf still want to kill me?"

"No," Darian said the pang of guilt he felt growing.

"May I watch you shift? I'd like to thank your spirit wolf for protecting me." She glanced around at the pack who listened intently to every word she was saying. "Unless, that's not a good idea?"

Darian nodded as he searched for his voice. "It is a great idea. My wolf will never hurt you. You don't have to be afraid of him."

"Because he's part of you?"

Darian swallowed hard as he nodded once again. His wolf pushing to be set loose. His instincts so basic that all he wanted to do was claim her as his mate. Darian mastered his wolf spirit and knew he would be in control. It was important that Cara trust his spirit wolf, if she didn't her spirit wolf wouldn't either.

The pack began to shift from their human forms into those of their wolf spirits. They understood what he was feeling, toward Cara and left to give them this moment alone.

All except for Ian as he'd promised to protect Cara.

Darian took several steps back. Before he allowed his wolf to push forward and shift his body into that of the wolf. He watched Cara as he changed, seeing himself through her eyes.

She pressed her hands over her mouth as his bones shifted and the cracking and stretching of his flesh began but as the white wolf emerged she lowered her hands from her mouth. Her blue eyes ran over Darian in a kind of awe that he knew he didn't deserve.

He planned to roll onto his back to show her he wouldn't hurt her but Cara fearless as ever approached him while he stood at his full height. Darian was no small wolf.

"Thank you for protecting me," she said and stretched her hand out and tentatively stroked his head.

Her touch inflamed his wolf's need to claim her but Darian held him back. Darian waited for Cara to remove her hand and back away. She didn't.

"You're so soft and beautiful," she said running her hand down his back. Darian's wolf shoved forward nuzzling Cara's hand without Darian's permission.

Darian pulled him back but Cara was smiling. Both her hands were on him. Her fingers rubbed his ear and it felt so good Darian became afraid he might lose control over his spirit wolf.

Her hands roamed over his chest and down his stomach as Darian's spirit wolf nuzzled against her shamelessly.

"You should probably let him go and run," Ian told Cara. His voice sounding much more like a plea than a suggestion. Ian wasn't mated yet and the sexual need Darian was feeding out to the pack through the energy he emitted, had to be painful.

Cara removed her hands and it took everything Darian had not to growl at Ian and command him to leave. He had to think about Cara, not his own physical needs.

Run, Darian commanded his wolf.

CHAPTER 11

Darian raced away leaving Cara with Ian.

For some reason Ian seemed uncomfortable, so Cara took the chance to go and select clothes that would fit her better than the ones she'd taken from Darian's room. Ian showed her to the room and then left to give her privacy.

Cara thought she'd find a small closet with a few clothes to sift through but it wasn't like that at all. The wardrobe, as Ian called it was an entire room filled with clothing. Not just old clothing, or the standard issue that was handed out in Aldrich town, there were many colors and styles.

She found a dress that was a shade of pink she'd only ever seen in books. It was soft and delicate in shade and in texture. When Cara put it on loved it too much to take it off.

Never in her life had she experienced a material as soft and smooth as the dress. It wasn't loose and bulky like the dress she wore in Aldrich town. This one fit her like the clothes fit women in the books.

Her shape was defined with curves Cara never noticed that she had. The body of the skinny girl in a dress resembling a bag was nothing like the young woman she saw staring back at her in the mirror.

She wished that the purple and yellow swell on her cheek wasn't so pronounced. Cara also was seeing her short hack job on her hair for the first time. It was crooked and not especially flattering but she loved it.

It was the first step she took in defying and escaping Aldrich. Perhaps if she could straighten the cut it would be less distracting but she didn't miss the length that served as a rope for Aldrich.

There weren't any shoes and she noticed that none of the pack wore them. She supposed that she wouldn't need them after she shifted.

Satisfied with the dress she left the wardrobe finding Ian waiting just outside the door. He closed his eyes and let out a groan when she emerged.

"Is this wrong? Should I have picked pants?"

"You get to wear whatever you want, Cara. I don't know what kind of rules you had in Aldrich Town but here, you can't go wrong unless you do something to hurt the pack."

Cara smiled at that. "I wouldn't be punished for anything else? What about bathing? How often can I wash?"

Ian frowned. "You want to wash?"

"Yes. Why wouldn't I?"

"Because Aldrich town people smell like..." he swallowed remembering with whom he was speaking. "like they don't like to wash."

Cara lowered her gaze. "It's due to the water shortage." When she looked at Ian again his face was red with obvious remorse.

"I thought shifters didn't have emotions," Cara said in an effort to show him that she understood how easy it is to make assumptions and believe them.

"Really?"

"Yes, and I thought that when they were in the form of a human, that they still thought like a wild animal, a predator. Everyone in Aldrich Town is taught to believe it."

Ian frowned. "By Aldrich?"

"Not directly, but yes. Everything is done as Aldrich wants it done. It's his town." An awkward silence stretched after that statement so Cara changed the subject. "You closed your eyes when I came out in this dress. Will you tell me why?"

"Yeah. I closed my eyes because I know when Darian comes back and sees you in that dress he's going to struggle with his manly… needs."

Cara looked down at her dress. "His needs? Is that your way of saying sex?"

"Or you can call it mating. That's probably more appropriate a word for us to use so I get to keep my balls when Darian comes back."

Cara shrugged. "I asked Darian if he wanted to… mate when I first got here. He said that he didn't."

"That was not true and it was before he got to know you better."

"Now he needs to mate?"

Ian shrugged. "I'll let him answer you on that question."

"It is my duty to mate with him? Do all the females of the pack mate with him?"

"Nope." Ian answered backing away from Cara. "I should have made Kate stay with you."

Cara allowed him to back away, she didn't want to make him uncomfortable but she also needed to know what was expected of her. "Who does he mate with then?"

"Shifter wolves mate for life, so the answer to your question is no one else."

Cara looked down at her dress. If Darian left her in the forest she would have died, or been found by Aldrich. He saved her and if he needed to mate then she supposed she should allow him to do so, he'd already told her she was destined to mate with him, she just didn't think it was going to be so soon.

The word destined made it seem far off in the distance.

Her father made sure that Cara was untouched by other men. While she didn't know anything about sex first hand, her father paid for the use of some of the women in the town.

Cara knew from the way her father talked about it, and the way she heard other men talk about it, like Aldrich, that it was pleasurable for men. The women her father used didn't sound as though it was something they enjoyed.

They didn't look happy when they arrived at the house, they sounded like they were in pain, sometimes even crying, during mating and when they left it was not with a happy expression on their face.

Cara knew that eventually she would be expected to allow a man to take his pleasure with her. Thinking of Darian as that man she no longer dreaded it.

He would be as gentle as he could be and that warm, secure sensation she felt when he touched her would make it nice.

"Thank the Lord, Kate and Jules are back," Ian breathed heavily. As soon as the two women found them in the large sitting room Ian took Kate's word to protect Cara and bolted out of the house.

Jules scowled at Cara before disappearing into another part of the big fortress.

"Don't mind her," Kate said. "She thought she was going to be Darian's mate. She just needs time to accept it."

Cara felt a pang of something similar to anger but different. "Did Darian tell her she was his destined mate?"

"No. You don't have to worry about Darian having a wandering eye. He's quite taken with you." When Kate's statement eased that feeling away, Cara realized she was feeling jealous and perhaps territorial.

Or, is that my spirit wolf?

"Is there anything you'd like to do before going to bed?"

Cara reached up feeling the long slant of her hair. "Yes. Can you cut my hair? I did a terrible job of making it straight."

"I'd be happy to."

* * *

IT WAS WELL after midnight when Darian returned from the run. He was the last one to return to the Rizer community, but he wasn't about to return when he wanted so much to be with Cara. When his wolf was demanding, he claim her.

Darian ran his wolf hard. He ran himself until he was exhausted.

Once he shifted back into his human form and was dripping wet with sweat, he took a shower long enough to wash off and then dressed into new pants.

His heart was pounding so hard in his chest that he was sure he was waking the entire community of werewolves.

Just go inside.

Darian opened the door quietly and stepped inside, shutting the door behind himself. His eyes went straight to the bed where Cara lay. She was on the top of the blankets toward the left side of the big bed.

She was dressed in a pale pink dress that hiked up her thighs as Cara moved in sleep.

Shit.

Darian walked over to the bed and tossed the blanket from the right side over Cara's body.

This was nothing like what he felt when he first lusted after Cara. It was all about his physical response to her then, and much easier to deny. Now, it was about so much more than the physical. Darian wanted to fill her, take away that emptiness she didn't even realize she was carrying.

He wanted to show her how good his touch could be for her. Darian wanted Cara to yearn for his touch, crave it like he craved her.

That hiked up skirt was burned into his mind even with the blanket covering Cara. He wanted to kiss his way up her thighs and taste her.

His manhood was standing at attention and throbbing with his need to have her, to claim her as his own.

"Darian?"

"Yes, it's just me." He wiped his face with the back of his hand.

Cara pushed back the blanket. "You were gone a long time."

"I needed the exercise."

Her lips pressed together and she gave a sharp nod. Cara reached back and unbuttoned the dress. Darian held his breath in disbelief as the dress slid down her beautiful body.

Does she want this?

His cock was pressing so hard against the restraint of his pants that it was painful. Darian walked back around the bed to the side where she stood.

He could hear her heart beating wildly and knew she was afraid. "Cara, what are you doing?"

The blues of her eyes darted up to his face and then back down to his chest. She didn't say anything. Cara sat down on the bed and then lay down drawing her legs up on the bed as well.

She wants me to claim her.

Darian bent toward her his mouth watering to taste the sweet nectar between her parted legs.

Cara stiffened. Her muscles flexing as though she were preparing for a blow. Darian was only a breath from the pink rosette at her breast. If she was scared he could show her not to be afraid but this wasn't just fear.

Her eyes were blank and locked on the ceiling.

I can't take her like this.

Darian backed away from the bed until his heels hit the wall behind him.

"What's wrong?" Cara asked suddenly aware that he hadn't touched her.

"Why are you offering yourself to me?"

Cara looked down at her body and then quickly pulled the blanket up and over her nakedness. "I'm sorry."

Fucking hell. She's sorry?

"Cara, you don't want this so why are you doing this?"

She tucked the blanket in tighter around her body. "I am prepared to fulfill my responsibility. You said we're destined mates."

"Responsibility?"

"I thought this is what you wanted."

Darian pressed a hand over his rock-hard member thinking Cara couldn't possibly know how much he wanted her.

"Not like this."

He had to get out of there or he was going to do or say something he'd regret. "Cara, you misunderstood. Okay? I want you to go back to sleep."

"I don't know what I'm expected to do to fulfill my responsibility here. What is destined mate if it isn't an eventual mating of two people?"

"Cara, it shouldn't be something you have to do. It should be something you want to do. You have to want me Cara. Want me to touch you and taste you. You should want to spread your legs for me and need my dick thrusting into you."

This is why you should have left already, Darian. She's not ready for this.

She stared back at him. There were questions in her eyes but she said nothing.

Darian left the bedroom and woke Errol, Ian's twin. "Keep her safe."

"Where are you going?" Errol asked.

Darian didn't answer. He didn't know where he was going. He just knew he had to get far away or he was going to lose the battle with his wolf and end up in that room pulling back the cover from Cara and showing her what she'd been too afraid to ask.

CHAPTER 12

*D*arian didn't return for two days.

As soon he came back though, Cara felt his eyes on her before she saw him. She was so embarrassed over what she'd done she couldn't bear to look at him.

She'd offered him her body after he'd already told her he didn't want to be stuck being her destined mate. All that talk about refusing to mate with her because she didn't desire him was just an excuse. Women didn't get desire. Not like men.

He knew she would never come to him hoping he'd stab into her body with his. Why couldn't he just continue being honest with her? Why didn't he just admit that he didn't want to mate with her.

The pack greeted him and he asked them questions about the community and about Aldrich Town. He didn't ask about Cara. It was Jules who volunteered the information.

"She said you told her she could train to kill Aldrich. Rafi, and I have stepped up to make amends for our lack of support."

"Thank you, Jules. Darian," Cara heard him say.

When no one said anything else, Cara figured Darian was behind her as she picked at her lunch. A pull to turn around and greet him had Cara standing up.

Stop it. Cara scolded her spirit wolf.

"Are you going to welcome me back, Cara?" Darian asked. He was standing directly behind her as she suspected.

Cara knew if they were going to move past the embarrassment she had to face him. Her heart skipped a beat as she turned around to look at him.

I missed you.

"Welcome back," she said.

He was holding a brown bag in his hand and looking at her like maybe he missed her too. "I brought something back for you."

"From Aldrich Town?"

"No," Darian said. He reached out and took her hand. "I want to give it to you while we're alone.' He led her out of the dining room, across the courtyard and into a room that was not his. Darian led her past the bed and out a door at the back of the room.

Cara didn't explore each and every room yet and was surprised when they stepped out onto a private enclosed garden. "This is beautiful," Cara said forgetting that she was humiliated.

"I bought you this from a store in the city of Sacramento."

Cara smiled at the brown bag. "Is it a fully functional city?"

"Yes, one of many. I know when you climbed that mountain that you wanted to see something like Sacramento. You wanted to know that there is still hope for more than just existing." Darian handed Cara the bag. "I couldn't bring you back the city but I thought you might like this."

Cara smiled holding the bag in her lap and enjoying the anticipation of what might be inside the bag. Darian sat down next to Cara on the bench, his leg against hers. "Aren't you going to open it?"

"Yes, of course. Thank you for this gift."

"You don't know what it is yet."

Cara parted the bag and pulled out a round crystal bulb with a busy city inside. Tiny round balls of snow falling around the busy roads.

"It's beautiful. Does it look like this, Sacramento, I mean?"

"Yes. It still does."

She turned the bulb over and then back watching the snow fall again over the city. "Thank you. I love it."

"Do you?" He asked taking her hand in his again.

"Yes."

Darian smiled. "I'm glad."

"Don't worry," Cara said slipping her hand from his. "I understand what you were trying to say before. I won't do that again and put you in that position."

His smile fell. "I don't get the feeling you do know what I was saying."

Cara carefully wrapped the bulb of the snowing city in the bag. She wished he wouldn't demand going back over it all but, she supposed it would be best if he confirmed that he didn't want her.

"Tell me what you think I meant."

Her face burned but she refused to continue avoiding his gaze. "You don't want to mate with me."

"Yes, I do."

The heat in her cheeks stung with the added humiliation he was adding with his denial of the truth. "Women don't want men the way you said I would have to want you. It hurts for the woman during mating. I don't understand why you won't just admit that you don't want to mate."

"Cara, there is more than pain for the woman during mating. It feels good for the woman too."

Cara clenched her teeth. "I love this present. Thank you." She started to stand but Darian stopped her. "Jules told you that I'm training. I agreed to resume after lunch. I don't want to keep them waiting."

"They'll wait, Cara," Darian said.

She could see he was upset. The vein at his forehead was pulsing.

"Do you trust me at all?"

"Yes. I trust you when you said you'd let me leave if it was what I really wanted. I trust that you're going to let me help to fight Aldrich."

Darian's nostrils flared, his gold eyes intent on her face. "Will you trust me enough to show you that it doesn't all hurt?"

Cara stiffened, she couldn't help it. And she could see in Darian's eyes that it upset him to see her react the way she was. "How? Do you intend to mate with me out here?"

"I want you to let me touch you."

The look on Aldrich's face as his hands opened and closed when he'd ordered her to strip came to her mind making her feel sick.

He's not Aldrich.

"If you don't like it you can tell me to stop."

Cara didn't understand why he was insisting on this but it seemed important to him. "Okay."

Darian stood and closed the door leading back into the bedroom. When he returned, he straddled the bench as he sat down facing her. "Come here, Cara," he said and gathered her in his arms.

She waited for him to continue but he was just holding her.

"I know that a hug doesn't hurt," Cara said turning in his arms to unpeel his arms from around her. His arms tightened around her keeping her where she was.

"I'm just waiting for you to relax."

"Oh," Cara said. "I'm relaxed."

He exhaled and his hot breath tickled the skin on her neck. "No, you're not. You're tense. I won't hurt you."

Cara again remembered Aldrich and that look on his face.

"Stop it," Darian said surprising her. "Wherever you're going in that head of yours, stop it," he said his voice full of authority. "Look at me. Stay here in this moment with me and decide for yourself."

She nodded. "I'll try."

His eyes lowered to her mouth and he slowly came closer keeping eye contact with her until his lips touched hers. She nearly broke the kiss to tell him to stop making fun of her. She knew a kiss didn't hurt, but as he ran his tongue over her lower lip, Cara felt herself leaning into him.

Darian sank his fingers into her hair as he continued to kiss her. The sensation was like getting away with a stolen cookie, delicious and too good to feel sorry about it.

His tongue pushed inside her mouth and she opened up to him as his tongue caressed hers. An intimate caress she didn't know she'd like so much.

When his warm hand cupped her breast through the shirt she was wearing she drew back in surprise.

"Does this hurt, Cara?" He asked, his voice sounding oddly thick.

She looked down at his hand as his thumb began to circle the peak. It didn't hurt. In fact, it felt good and strange too. As if there was a string running from within her breast to the place between her legs. Every tug and pinch sending an electric pulse through the string.

"My father would kill me if he knew I was letting you touch me like this," Cara said surprised at how breathless she sounded.

"Your father will never raise a finger against you again. Forget him right now. Do you like the way this feels?"

Cara nodded.

"Good," he said in that same thick voice that made the center of her body begin to vibrate and stir. His hand remained on her breast but the other began to open the buttons of her shirt.

She sat up a little straighter. Cara looked at his face trying to stay in the moment and not think about anything else. He was looking at his hand with a warm honey hue to his golden eyes. His eyes met hers as he lowered his head. His mouth closed around her nipple. His hot tongue flicking her tight bud as he sucked her into his mouth.

The string inside was on fire with heat and electrified sensations that she didn't know what to do with. She gasped as she continued to watch him sucking on her breast.

"Darian," she gasped as that feeling continued to intensify. His mouth crossed to her other breast where he sucked and licked her with long hungry strokes. That feeling was growing stronger, it was good but it also felt like some kind of pressure.

"You're so beautiful, Cara. Mmm," he said sucking her deeper into his mouth. "You taste so good."

Her breathing was coming even faster.

"Darian, something's wrong."

He withdrew from her breast. "Does it hurt?"

"I don't know. It's kind of like raw nerves gathering."

Darian made a groaning sound as he clenched his teeth together. His hand ran up her thigh and rounded over the mound between her legs. "Here?" He asked.

Cara nodded. The heat of his hand was penetrating her pants and panties and the feeling was still growing.

"That's good."

"It feels like it's getting too tight," Cara breathed.

"Fuck, Cara, you're going to make me come in my pants," he said as his hand began to squeeze her.

Cara pressed her legs together when he unbuttoned the button on her pants. "Wait, I thought you were just going to touch."

"I am," He said as he pushed and pulled her knees open until she was sitting with her legs spread apart. Darian slid his hand under her panties and his fingers slid in between her folds.

She started closing her legs, knowing she really shouldn't be allowing him to touch her there.

Darian set his over her leg and in between her feet, effectively holding her open for his fingers to continue exploring her most intimate center.

His fingers circled and teased the sensitive nub at her core, pulling that string so tight it felt close to breaking. Cara grabbed his wrist to pull his hand out, but he was too strong. His teeth were clenched so tight as he continued massaging her. "Trust me, Cara."

She tried to wiggle away. The feeling was too strong. It was going to hurt when the string broke.

"Cara, look at my hand buried under your panties. You like the way that feels, don't you?"

Her hips pressed forward against his hand as the string pulled tighter and the nerves nearly burned with sensitivity.

"You're so wet for me Cara. You're making me thirsty." He lifted Cara up onto her feet, and pulled her pants and panties from her waist to her ankles.

She lowered her hands trying to cover herself as he lifted her again. This time when he pushed her legs apart he had her sitting on his hands as he lowered her onto his mouth.

Cara gasped as his tongue delved between her slick folds. He groaned against her as his hot tongue explored her with a hunger that felt so good it snapped the string.

Her body seemed to burst from the inside out in hot, delicious, pulsing, demanding, sensations that pulled a cry from her as she watched him kissing, and eating her into a magic kind of bliss that obliterated all coherent thought.

Slowly the amazing, all-encompassing, ecstasy calmed to a feeling of deep satisfaction. Darian lowered her gently back down onto his lap. The warm honey of his eyes now a smoldering gold melting pot.

He gathered her close as they both tried to catch their breath.

"I'm glad you trusted me Cara."

She smiled against his chest.

Me too.

CHAPTER 13

Touching Cara, teaching her about her body and how good it could feel was nearly the undoing of Darian's control. Somehow, he'd managed not to finish what he'd started, at least for himself. His cock was so rock hard, his desire to sink his shaft into the heat of her center was strong enough to make his body shake.

Never in his entire existence did he want anyone or anything as much as he wanted Cara. His love for Cara was the only possible entity powerful enough to stop him and his wolf from taking her. Her trust in him was more important.

So, Darian held her until her breathing slowed and her heartbeat returned to its steady pace. Her smile and the sated look in her eyes warmed his heart.

"You should go and meet with Jules, and Rafi," Darian said.

Cara nodded and climbed from his lap.

Darian gripped the bench so hard it began to crack as he watched her bend to retrieve her clothing. He closed his eyes knowing he was still in danger of losing control.

Don't ruin this. Let her walk away remembering only how good I made her feel.

"Darian?"

"Yes?" he asked.

"What's wrong?"

He opened his eyes. Thankfully Cara was dressed. "Nothing. Nothing at all."

"I apologize for not believing you."

Darian shook his head. "I know you must have had your reasons. I'm pleased you allowed me to show you."

Cara's cheeks blushed a lovely shade of pink. "I am too," She said cradling the snow globe he'd given her in her arms. She bent forward and kissed his cheek. She dashed away back through the bedroom and out into the courtyard.

Darian stalked through the house and to his bedroom. If he didn't do something about the steel rod between his legs he was going to get mean, and his wolf was only going to become so obsessed with claiming Cara that he'd be fighting Darian for control every second of every day until he claimed Cara.

In his bedroom where it still carried Cara's scent from sleeping in his bed he remembered the sweet taste of her, the feel of her slippery heat, and imagined how it would feel when he would thrust inside her. How she would gasp and look at him with the desire she'd shown him only moments ago.

Claim her. His wolf demanded. *She's ours.*

He pumped his hand up and down his cock. Replaying the way she'd watched him kissing and sucking on her breasts. The surprise of every sensation that he stirred within her. Then he thought of the way she'd rolled her hips pressing her pussy against his mouth as she came.

At last the surge release found him. His hand holding still as he pumped his cock through his grip imagining he was inside of Cara and she was begging for him not to stop. He finished with a groan of relief.

He cleaned up and then took a shower. The edge of his need was at least taken down several notches but the relief he felt was short lived.

Claim her. His wolf demanded. *Claim her before it's too late.*

* * *

"You have to block those," Jules said as Cara pushed up off the stone floor of the courtyard. Her lungs were still struggling to fill with air after the powerful kick Jules delivered to her sternum. It'd knocked the wind right out of her.

Rafi stepped between Cara and Jules. "Ease up, Jules." His gaze hard on the other woman.

"We can take a break if you think she needs it. I was only trying to help. Aldrich isn't going to be gentle with her if Darian ever let's her go near Aldrich town again."

Cara sucked in a full breath at last and the dizziness began to pass.

"He isn't going to let her," Rafi said.

"Why are we training her then? I thought that was the whole point of what we're doing here."

Cara nodded still trying to find her voice. "Darian said I could stay. I could train." She gasped for another breath. "He said I can help stop Aldrich."

Jules laughed a mean sound. A taunting sound that reminded Cara of Aldrich. "He said you can help. That's not the same as letting you come with us. If you pack Darian a lunch it'll be helping. Don't you see?"

Cara shook her head. "Darian doesn't play games like that with me. He doesn't think like you do."

Rafi smiled at Cara and laughed at the angry expression that sharpened Jules features. "She can't help but see the best in him. So soon after such an experience, anyway."

Cara scowled at Rafi.

"Don't be mad," he said still smiling. "I wasn't spying on you or anything."

"Then how-"

Jules cut in. "We can smell it. We're wolves. Remember?"

Cara lowered her eyes hating the way Rafi was looking at her and the way her face was burning. She felt humiliated and exposed. "What happened between Darian and me does not factor into what I've said. I know Darian will keep his word to me and I don't appreciate either of you commenting on matters that are private."

Rafi's smile shrank to a straight line, his dark eyes avoiding Cara's.

Good.

"I bet you are thirsty. I'll get you something to drink," Rafi said leaving Jules and Cara alone in the courtyard.

Jules exhaled as she rotated her pointed shoulders. "I'm sorry that I embarrassed you. I know exactly how you feel."

"You do?"

"Yes. When Darian and I were messing around together I knew the whole pack could practically taste how wet Darian got me. His mouth feels so good. Doesn't it?"

What a bitch.

Cara latched onto Darian's assurances that Jules was jealous of Cara's position as his destined mate and held on tight. She knew that if she was in Aldrich Town, her escort would not allow her to fight back or say anything to anyone who was unkind or trying to upset her.

But she wasn't in Aldrich Town. Not anymore.

Remind her where she stands. She stands beneath us.

Cara felt stronger, brave with her wolf spirit stand with her. She looked Jules dead in the eye taking four steps to cross through the distance that stood between them.

Jules cocked her head to the side staring back at Cara. "I just kicked your ass. Do you really want to try and face me down?"

"Absolutely."

Jules' lips pinched together as her green eyes widened. "I can't help it that Darian and I have a past together."

"You are lying."

"You're angry because you know that I'm not lying. You're not special to him. You're his job."

Silence her lies.

Her arms pushed out before she could think and sent Jules sliding across the stone floor. Cara looked down at her hands in surprise.

How did I do that?

"Great progress, Cara," Rafi cheered as he returned to the courtyard. He handed Cara the water. "You missed it," he called out as Darian entered the courtyard from the opposite side. "She's coming along well. We can go after him in a matter of days."

"Go after him?" Darian asked drawing closer to Cara and Rafi.

Cara nodded. "Yes, like you promised. You said I can stay and help stop Aldrich."

"You can," Darian said his words coming out chopped and tight. "Not in a few days. You can help after you shift."

"Right," Jules said as she picked herself up. "She can lead the pack with you. With two alphas Aldrich won't be able to escape us."

Cara caught the way his mouth tightened as he listened to what Jules said. "Cara will still need to learn how to work with her spirit wolf."

"Are you saying I won't get to fight him?" Cara asked. There was too much he wasn't saying. It was like he was avoiding answering the question.

"Cara... I promised you I would never let him hurt you. I can't allow you to be anywhere near him."

You lied to me.

The burn of betrayal fueled her temper. "You said I could help stop him."

"And you will." He reached for her but Cara slapped his hands away.

"How?"

"You're going to tell us his schedule, his movements in the town. You can tell us if there are any weak points in the wall, or if there are any allies on the inside we can contact to help us."

The burn lessened as he spoke. It was more than Jules described but still less than what Cara wanted. "I can do more than that."

"As much as you like," Darian agreed this time taking hold of her and dragging her close to him. "As long as you are nowhere near, Aldrich."

Cara glared at him. "Don't tell me what I can and can't do, Darian."

"Don't make me break my promise and forbid you, Cara. I know he's hurt you. I know you want justice but I also know that the man himself is poison. He isn't done trying to hurt you and I'll be damned if I give him the chance."

CHAPTER 14

Cara continued training with Rafi and Jules. After Darian walked away. She didn't argue with Darian because she didn't want him to use his alpha authority to command her to stay but she had no intention of standing on the sidelines again and hoping someone else would step up and stop Aldrich.

When training was finished, Cara was dripping with sweat but she was still angry with Darian.

"I just wish we could get her to Aldrich before she shifted."

"Why?" Cara asked butting into Jules and Rafi's conversation.

Jules grunted. "It doesn't matter. We can't do that."

"Why do you wish we could go before I shift?" Cara asked again.

"You're still immune to the poison. You won't be after you shift," Jules said. "Getting Aldrich has been impossible because he doesn't leave. Getting him means getting inside."

Cara rolled the statement around in her mind. She didn't trust either of them to just believe what they said, but this statement, it fit with the things Darian said about the poison and about Aldrich.

"I'll have to change his mind," Cara decided aloud.

"He's not going to change his mind. He's stubborn," Jules said.

Cara nodded. "Yeah, but I'm ten times worse."

With her plan forming in her mind Cara left Rafi and Jules staring after her. She went to the wardrobe room and took her time finding items she hoped would aid her plan.

After bathing she dressed in the stretchy, form fitting, lavender dress. Then she brushed out her short hair and looked herself over in the mirror. "Not bad."

We look good.

Cara smiled. Kate was right about growing to love her spirit wolf. Cara liked her more and more with each passing day.

She found Darian helping to set the table.

Tonight, was a formal night. Not every dinner with the pack was eaten at the table. Sometimes, they took the food outside and ate either on blankets or on the grass. Cara loved it most when they got to eat outside but tonight, eating inside suited her plan best.

"You look beautiful," Darian said when he saw her. "Are you still angry with me?"

"Yes," Cara said. "But not terribly furious. Do you know why?"

He smiled drawing closer to her. "Why?"

"Because I know how I'm going to change your mind."

His smile seemed to flip over as he frowned. "You won't change my mind."

"I didn't learn a lot of useful information in Aldrich Town but there is one thing that I know to be true."

"What's that?"

Cara leaned on the bravery of her spirit wolf and took a step toward him. She reached up and put her hands on the back of his neck guiding him toward her.

Her heart hammered in her chest as she recognized that heated gold hue in his gaze. Avoiding his kiss, she whispered in his ear, "Men are driven by sex. They need it. They crave it and when they want it most is when they can't have it at all."

"Cara," her name sprang from his lips in a warning tone.

"I refuse to mate with you until you agree that I can fight Aldrich."

Darian growled a deadly sound but Cara wasn't afraid of him. She released her hold on him and kissed his cheek as she began pulling back.

Darian reached out and caught her hand before she could dash away. "You want to kiss me Cara? Kiss me." He took her mouth with his. His lips heated like his gaze. Her body seemed to melt against his with the heat. His hand cupped her breast through the thin material of the dress.

Cara arched her back pressing into his hand as her nipples hardened with anticipation.

Then he let go of her hand and her breast pulling abruptly away from her lips. "Two can play at this game, Cara.

CHAPTER 15

"She's killing me," Darian admitted to Killian.

"Why not claim her?" Killian asked. "It's clear she loves you."

Darian barked out a laugh. "She loves me? The woman wants me to die of an aneurism."

Killian shook his head. "I don't see how-"

"Last week she reached under the table and stroked my dick until I was so hard, I could have drilled a hole through our table."

Killian's dark brows rose. "And you just let her?"

"I returned the favor, but… The more I touched her…"

"I'm actually surprised you didn't give in that night," Killian admitted. "Is that the last time she tried to get you to fold?"

I wish.

"I've been sleeping in the office. It's the only way I can be sure I won't give in during a weak moment."

Killian exhaled shaking his head with a smile on his face that pissed Darian off.

"Are you going to help me or not?"

"You are the *alpha*. You don't need my help."

Darian growled with his wolf. "I look forward to the day you fall in love Killian. I'm going to laugh in your face, you know that?"

"I'm not the mate for life type. Sorry."

"I cannot command her to submit. You can't be that stupid when it comes to women, Killian."

Killian laughed. "I probably am but that isn't what I meant."

"Well? What did you mean?"

"She's in love with you. Tell her how you feel and let her love for you make up her mind for her."

Darian rubbed his eyes. He was so tired. Sleep was impossible to find because his body was in a constant state of arousal and need. "I hope you're right."

"We all do. You two are a permeating aphrodisiac walking around. It's putting me in a really shitty mood, Darian. Like I said, I'm not the mate for life kind."

Darian left Killian's office and found Cara training with Rafi, and Jules. Cara was working hard. That look of solid determination on her face was the same as the one she'd worn when she made that leap, climbing the mountain.

"Leave us," Darian roared as he stalked to the center of the courtyard where Cara stood.

She was breathing hard as he approached. Her pupils dilating as she looked up at him. "Had enough?"

"Have you?"

"You have to let me fight him. You have to let me face him. Don't you understand that I can't live with what I've already done? I stood by and did nothing. I have to *do* something. It has to stop."

Darian reached for her ignoring her hands as she swatted against his hands and pulled her into an embrace. "None of that has anything to do with the fact that we're denying ourselves each other. I want to marry you Cara. I want to protect you and keep you safe."

"And you want-"

"Yes," he growled. "I want to make love to you, Cara. I want to belong to you as I feel you do to me. We are predestined. Fated. I know you feel it."

Cara pushed away from him. Tears slid down her face. "It's all I have to make you listen to me. I want you like I was never supposed to want anyone. If you love me even half as much as I love you then you'll let me go after Aldrich."

Darian's forehead creased as he studied her. "You mean to go after him yourself? By yourself?"

"Yes," Cara said the sweet vulnerability she'd given him a glimpse of disappearing as her determination pushed to the front. "He won't expect that I would kill him. He's wrong."

CHAPTER 16

*C*ara woke in Darian's bed once again finding herself alone. Two weeks of pleading with him, begging him, touching him, trying to tempt him and Darian had the same answer for her.

Today will be different. She told herself as she climbed out of the bed. Cara was sore from training and she was sad because she thought that by now Darian would understand.

She didn't see him at breakfast.

He's avoiding me again.

Cara met Jules and Rafi for a run. It was supposed to build up her endurance but today they didn't push too hard. It wasn't a day to overdo.

They didn't talk much. Cara was nervous. Her window of opportunity to get into Aldrich town was closing. Soon she would shift and the chance to end the terror he inflicted would be gone.

After lunch, they worked on training again. Cara thought she would not see him at all and hated that her insides ached and hurt with how much she missed him.

It wasn't until she was eating dinner that she felt his gaze on her. She turned around finding him standing on the second floor. Cara could see him through the window of his bedroom.

I love you.

She swallowed the ache in her throat as she remembered what he'd said to her when he'd pleaded with her to stop the standoff. He looked as alone as she felt.

Darian, I love you. Why can't you trust me to be brave enough to stand against Aldrich?

As if he could hear her thoughts, Darian turned away from the window, leaving his bedroom.

He'd go back to his office, where he'd have tea and arrange for more supplies to be delivered from their allies in Sacramento. He clung to pack business waiting her out.

The pack began to shift to go for their evening run. Tonight, they were combing the mountainside behind the Rizer Fortress.

Cara returned to the community with Jules and Rafi. Her hands were sweating as she tugged at the skirt of the thin pink dress she loved so much.

"Here you go," Jules said handing Cara the teacup and saucer.

She took it from Jules and went to his office before she lost her nerve. Turning the handle, Cara pushed the door open and walked entered without knocking.

"Your tea," Cara bit out setting the cup in front of him on his desk.

Darian's jaw clenched as he gave a sharp nod. "Thank you."

Cara remained where she was waiting for him to look at her.

"Is there something else?" He asked tightly, still not looking up at her.

"I'm waiting for the teacup."

Darian lifted the cup of hot tea and tossed it back like a shot of strong alcohol. "There." He nearly broke the cup as he smacked it against the saucer.

"Let me go after, Aldrich."

"No."

Cara slammed the office door shut still standing inside with Darian. "Who are you to decide what I will do? I shouldn't need your permission." She slammed her hands down on his desk.

Darian looked up from the paperwork at last.

. . .

EVERY TIME he looked at her, his body grew hard. The sound of her voice made his shaft thicken, and the way she licked her lips made him crave the feel of her skin against his lips.

"Please, Darian. Seven years of my life he's stolen, keeping us in that cage. You don't know what it's like not to feel the sun on your face for days at a time."

Darian stood leaning over the desk to meet her gaze. "You're right. I wouldn't have survived if I were put in so small a space. It is unspeakable what Aldrich has done and is still doing to the people of the town. But, Cara. You have suffered enough. *Leave him to me.*"

"You've had seven years to get to him," she challenged. "Tell me what I have to do to prove to you I can do this."

A million sexual requests shot through his mind as he met that warrior fire in her eyes. He would not ask for any of them. Nothing was more important than keeping her safe. "You have too many scars already. I will not allow you to be hurt again."

"Jules thinks I can do it," Cara said as he rounded the desk heading for the door.

Of course, she did.

Darian turned back around and took a step back into the office. "Jules wants you out of her way so she can try and be the wolf at my side. You can't believe a word she says."

Cara folded her arms. "Why not? At least she's talking to me."

"I'm talking to you, Cara. I'm just not giving you your way," Darian said closing the space between them. "I've been holding back. Enduring all your teasing without pushing you to the brink as you've done to me."

Cara licked her lips the blue in her eyes brightening as he wrapped his arm around her waist. Darian framed her face with his other hand and claimed her lips with his. She was stiff under him, fighting what he knew she felt too.

So, bloody stubborn.

He swept his tongue over the seam of her lips, loving the taste of her. She was just as sweet as her scent. Darian tilted her head to get better access to her mouth. As he tried again to get her to open to him.

When he sucked her bottom lip into his mouth, and pulled her firmly against him. His hard and shaft pressing against her soft flesh.

Cara gasped.

The whimper of sound coming from Cara reminded him of her fear, and her innocence. He began to withdraw from her slowly. Darian could feel her tongue moving with his. He couldn't take what she wasn't willingly giving.

"Cara," he said her name, his voice thick with his desire for her.

"Did you touch Jules like you touch me?" Cara asked him, her voice quiet.

"No," Darian answered. "There is no one else but you, Cara."

Her breasts were rising and falling with each breath she took. Her nipples were tight and pressed against bodice of her dress, calling to him to be tasted, touched, and teased.

I don't know how much longer I can stop myself from claiming her. Please Cara, tell me you want this. You want me.

He looked at her with desire in his eyes. Cara didn't feel nervous or afraid that he might try and force himself on her. She knew he wouldn't.

Darian, said things to her that made her feel beautiful and loved. It was the kind of things she'd longed to have said to her. He cared about her, and was gentle with her.

The connection they shared through their spirit wolves gave her a glimpse of what he was feeling for her and the sensation of devotion and love humbled her. She'd been cold with him all this time and now that she wanted to respond to him she didn't know what to do.

"If I... if we mate, will you let me train to lead the pack with you against Aldrich?"

"No," he answered without hesitation. "I love you. There is nothing anyone could give me that would make me change my mind and allow Aldrich to be anywhere near you."

His strong, protective tone heated her from the inside out. She wanted to kiss him, to have his hands on her body, to feel his skin against hers.

Cara walked over to the door Darian left open and pulled it shut. She wasn't sure what to do or say. She only knew that she wanted to be with Darian, she wanted to experience what it felt like to be loved.

"I mean what I said, Cara. You will not return to Aldrich town. It is far too dangerous."

She took a few steps toward him, but her knees started to shake with fear and nervousness, so, she stopped. Her fingers found the top button on the front of the dress. She undid the button, reminding him of the first time she'd stripped for him.

The vein in his forehead stood out further as his golden eyes watched her fingers. "I want you so much that I can barely breath, Cara. But I won't have you this way."

Cara gulped, her fingers catching and accidentally releasing the second button.

"Please, Cara. I am Alpha but I am still a man. You are pushing me too far."

Cara lowered her gaze and could see the evidence of his arousal, straining against his pants. His hand wrapped around the edge of the desk as she looked at him. He was growing longer and harder under her gaze.

It has to be tonight, Cara. Her spirit wolf urged.

"Darian, I know you won't give me permission or help me to get Aldrich myself."

His golden eyes concentrated on her face, he was trying so hard to keep from looking lower where her luscious curves called to him.

Maybe I'm not doing this right?

Cara walked across the room, ignoring the way her legs seemed to wobble with each step. "Kiss me?"

Darian was looking at her like he wasn't sure if he'd heard her correctly. Then he asked, "Where would you like me to kiss you, Cara?"

Everywhere.

"Wherever you like," Cara said to his chest. She was too afraid to look him in the eyes and see him laughing at her. This seduction thing wasn't as easy as she'd thought it would be.

Darian dipped his head. His soft black hair caressing her cheek as he passed her waiting lips. His hot mouth kissed her breast, sucking her tight bud deeply into his mouth through the material of the dress. Her fingers tangled in his hair as her mouth fell open.

He moaned a sound against her breast that shot heat down her body and wet heat blossomed between her legs.

His hands parted the V shaped opening, popping off the remaining buttons. They scattered across the floor as his tongue swept over her breast, his lips blazing a trail on her sensitive skin.

Watching him taste her, suck on her sent another electric wave of heat down her body. She squeezed her legs together at the overwhelming sensation.

"Cara, tell me to stop now if you want me to stop," he pleaded. "I want you so much. I'm afraid I won't be able to stop if you wait much longer to tell me you don't want to let me claim you tonight."

He was looking at her wet breasts, moist from his hungry mouth.

"Tell me what to do," Cara said. "I don't know what to do."

"Are you sure this is what you want? To be mine?"

Cara smiled down at the kindest, most powerful man she'd ever known. "Yes. I love you."

Darian swept her up in his arms as he stood. He kissed her as he carried her out into the hallway and into his room at top speed, it made her dizzy. His bed was beneath her so fast she had the sensation of falling but in his arms, she wasn't afraid.

"Pull up your dress for me, Cara" he said cupping her breasts.

Cara reached down and slid the skirt of the dress up her legs, over her thighs. His eyes were watching with baited anticipation. She pulled the dress off over her head.

Darian made a guttural, growling sound of approval as he looked at the soft down of her golden curls.

She knew that having sex was painful for the woman and Cara braced herself as he lowered over her. His mouth pressing wet hot kisses down her stomach.

"What are you doing?"

"I want to taste you, Cara. All of you." His eyes were locked with hers as he nuzzled the apex of her legs with his mouth. His tongue delved hungrily between her folds, reminding her how good he could make her feel. The sweet vibrations of his groan against her sensitive flesh had her pressing against his mouth.

Darian shoved down his pants kicking them to the floor. "I want to be inside you. Open your legs for me?" he asked.

Cara opened her knees and gasped at the sensation caused by Darian's cock rubbing over her clit and teasing her entrance. The heated push of his rounded member pressing at her opening intensified the ache for him. "I want you inside me, Darian," Cara breathed.

"Slowly, my love. I don't want to hurt you."

"Please, Darian. Don't make me wait," she pleaded.

His jaw clenched as the head of his cock pressed harder into her opening, slowly stretching the walls of her sex to accept him. She felt herself growing wetter as he continued to slowly stretch her. It was an intrusion but it felt so good. It was like he was filling the emptiness that ached for him, was missing him all this time.

Cara moved trying to take him in deeper. He backed away. "It will hurt if I do this too fast."

"I'm not afraid of the pain anymore."

"Does it hurt?" he asked, the strain on his face from his efforts to go slow showing in the tightness of his features and the pulsing vein on his forehead.

Cara moved against him again. "It feels so good, I can't hardly breathe. Darian, I need you."

He swore, his hips bucking against her.

She maneuvered her hips as he ground against her, guiding his cock into her core. He was buried inside her filling her, the tiny pinch of pain immediately replaced with the feeling of completeness.

Darian's mouth opened in disbelief. He couldn't believe she'd guided him inside of her when he knew how afraid she was of the pain. His dick pulsed inside her, the need to pound into her pussy too strong. Darian couldn't stop himself from thrusting into her wet heat holding him so tight.

Cara wrapped her legs around his waist, holding on as the delicious tangle of nerves tightened with need. She met each of his thrusts wanting more.

"You feel so good," he growled into her ear. His cock delving deeper into her heat. Cara gasped, her nails biting into his back and he stretched her deeper than she thought possible.

Suddenly the pressure seemed to explode where they were joined together, in wave after wave of pleasure. Her hips rocked against his, her back arching as she cried out.

Darian pressed deeper, a liquid heat filling her as he came deep inside her. He was looking at her with love, and lust as he rocked into her, loving the way her tight glove squeezed every drop from his cock into her pussy.

Rolling them both onto their sides, he kissed her. "I love you, Cara. Let's never go another day without doing that again." He was still holding her close.

Cara swallowed the lump of emotion swelling in her throat and kissed him as her answer.

"I will always love you and protect you, Cara."

She snuggled up against his heated body, hiding her face from his view. "I love you too," she said. "You know, If I'd known you were out here all this time, beyond the wall. I would have come to you sooner."

He blinked slowly, his eye lids heavy.

"I would have come for you if I'd known you were inside."

Cara kissed him again.

Don't come for me, Darian. It's too dangerous

CHAPTER 17

*J*ust like Jules said, Darian fell asleep about an hour after he drank the tea Jules spiked with a sleeping tonic of Killian's. Cara felt so much guilt as she disentangled herself from the man who was now her husband.

She'd tried to get him to see what had to be done but he loved her too much to let her go back.

He's going to be so angry when he wakes up and discovers what I've done.

Cara kissed him gently on the lips praying it wouldn't be their last kiss. She dressed into new clothes. The blue dress with the short sleeves and low cut neckline would serve her best. Aldrich would look at her in it and see the scared woman he was so bent on breaking.

Her heart pounding, she tip-toed from the room, leaving Darian asleep and alone in the bed.

Jules waited in the courtyard. Her green eyes looked black in the evening light. "Ready?"

Cara nodded.

Rafi bowed his head to her and then slowly Jules did too. "What are you doing? We have to go before he wakes up," Cara said.

"You are the female alpha now. We are showing you our respect."

"I'm just me. The same woman I was an hour ago."

Jules shook her head. "Nope. There's a big difference now. You belong to Darian. He'll break our necks when he hears we took you back to Aldrich Town."

"We've been over this. I'm the only one who can get inside. I haven't turned yet. The poison for the werewolves won't work on me."

"You sure you have what it takes to kill him?" Rafi asked. The worry on his face giving her little reassurance.

Cara nodded even though she wasn't so sure. The will to kill him? Yes. Did she have the strength to fight him? Probably not. She had to take him by surprise, it was the only way.

"Here, take this. All you need to do is cut him, just once and the poison on the blade will kill him." Rafi handed Cara a sheathed knife with a leg strap. The blade appeared to be the size of an envelope opener. Cara lifted her skirt and strapped the knife high on her thigh.

"This way, let's go," Jules whispered.

Cara followed Jules, and Rafi followed behind. It was just after sunset, not quite dark. The forest ahead thick with shadows made Cara's heart pound faster.

Quit being scared, Cara. You have to do this. Think of Uncle Mortimer and his family. Aldrich will have made someone pay for my escape. I have to end this.

Cara had to run to keep up with Jules. Rafi was right behind her. She was breathing hard, not sure how far they'd gone or how far they still had to go. Cara just knew that she was getting tired.

When Jules slowed to a stop in front of her, Cara was prepared to take another tongue lashing. "I'm pushing myself as fast as I can go," Cara said.

Jules held up her hand. She leaned forward tilting her head to the side.

She is listening, Cara realized.

Jules looked back at Rafi with a shrug. His shoulders were rising and his head lowering and his eyes had shifted into those of his grey and black wolf.

Cara couldn't hear anything beyond her heart pounding and her heavy breathing.

"It's just the elk. Don't you smell them?" Jules asked him.

"Get down, Cara," Rafi growled, his voice vibrating with a snarl as he began to shift. Black and gray fur spread out over his skin as he fell forward on to his hands. His growl was deafening as his bones shifted under the fur.

Cara dropped onto her stomach. Scanning the forest for any sign of danger. The broken dried leaves fluttered up and around her face as her heavy breathing stirred them and dust into the air.

Two men from Aldrich town raced out of the darkness. Their faces were twisted with fear and hatred. "No, wait," Cara cried out. The silver spears they were carrying were aimed at Rafi.

One of the hunters threw his spear and it stuck into the ground where Cara last saw Rafi.

Where is he?

A female cry sliced through the air. Cara pushed up onto her knees. She turned toward the scream in time to see Aldrich standing behind Jules. A silver spear protruding from her chest. Jules let out one last whimper as Aldrich bit into her neck.

The dark eyes of Aldrich were on Cara. He was enjoying the horror on her face. Cara shuddered with disgust. Tears burned her eyes as Jules stared blankly. She was gone.

He'll never stop killing. I have to end this.

Cara remained on her knees. She had to make him think she was weak. That she wouldn't fight him.

Aldrich dropped Jules to the ground. He stomped his booted foot into her back and pulled out the spear. "Come out and play, Rafi," Aldrich called, his voice full of anticipation. "You've killed the hunters. Aren't you coming for me?"

Cara kept her eyes on Aldrich. If Rafi killed both the hunters, he'd delivered a swift and silent death to both men.

He must be hiding in the shadows.

Cara couldn't see him, but she knew he wouldn't leave. He would never pass up the chance to kill Aldrich.

Aldrich pulled something from his pocket as he came toward her.

"Did you really think you could escape me? Leave me? You belong to me, Cara. Your life is *mine* to take."

Cara pushed up to her feet. The silver spear was at her chest before she could make a move for the knife hidden below the skirt of her dress. He pressed it forward, the tip pierced her dress and skin.

She cried out from the pain. It didn't just hurt, it burned like fire. Her body was already becoming affected by the silver.

A blur of movement behind Aldrich came to a sudden stop as Rafi dropped to the ground. His body stiff, as though he'd been flash frozen mid step.

"Like it?" Aldrich asked Cara holding a small tube. "Paulina helped me to perfect it." Faster than was humanly possible Aldrich snaked out a hand, grabbing a fistful of Cara's short hair. He dragged her forward until his face was only a few inches from hers. "I made special bullets, filled them with my own special brew of poison."

His hand in her hair jerked to the side, forcing Cara to look at Rafi.

"Is it he, who ravished your body? Did he tell you he loves you, Cara? I can smell it all over you. Wet dog."

Cara was inching her dress up her side. She needed to get to the knife. Glaring at him she refused to answer.

"You could save him. Do you realize that? Look," he gestured to Rafi with his pointer finger. The nail filed into a long sharp point.

Cara spotted the capsule stuck in Rafi's shoulder.

"With every moment that passes, the pain increases," Aldrich laughed. "The paralytic makes it impossible for him to remove the capsule that is leaking more and more of the poison into his body. I laced his with silver, regular poison won't kill a werewolf."

He yanked her hair again, pulling her head back as he ran his tongue over the bloody hole in her dress, and up her neck. His tongue was like wet sandpaper on her skin leaving a burning, raw trail in its wake.

Aldrich groaned a sickening sound of pleasure.

Cara finally had the skirt pulled up high enough she could reach the sheath. She unfastened the sheath and pulled the knife from the holster.

Bringing the knife up, she felt it hit something hard.

Aldrich, looked down where the knife cut through the shirt but no further. He gripped her wrist and twisted with crushing pressure. Cara screamed, holding on to the knife as long as she could. She could feel her wrist beginning to break. Her fingers filled with a tingling sensation, weakening her already precarious hold on her only weapon.

The knife fell, sticking in the dirt.

Aldrich continued to twist. "Now you remember who I am. I am king. Your master. Beg me for forgiveness," he growled.

Never.

Cara spat in his face. "You are nothing to me."

He roared like a feral animal. He let go of her wrist to grip her neck with both of his huge hands. "I'm everything," he told her as he squeezed.

"Aldrich, you've come out of your hiding place?" It was Darian, she knew his voice.

Aldrich loosened his grip on her neck. His black eyes widened with fear. "I'll snap her neck," Aldrich said. "I'll do it." Aldrich maneuvered her so that her back was against his chest, with one arm around her neck as he began to dig in his pocket.

"He's got a gun," Cara cried out trying to warn Darian.

The arm around her neck tightened cutting off her air again.

"All Valor had to do was bite me and none of this would have happened," Aldrich growled.

Darian's golden eyes were holding hers as he came out of the shadows. He seemed to say, *I'm coming for you. Don't be afraid*, without words.

"Save this innocent girl, Darian," Aldrich yelled, that same fear apparent in his voice. "Lay down and show me you'll let me take her home. Her father missed her so much he died, but her uncle and cousins are still waiting for her to come back."

My father is dead?

The darkness seemed to be getting darker. Her legs were growing weak.

"She's fading fast, Darian."

You're still standing by. Do something.

Cara let go of the arm around her neck. She reached back where she could feel him hiding the gun. She yanked it from his hand tossing the gun away.

Aldrich's arm around her neck tightened for an instant and then was gone.

Cara landed on her hands and knees. She was still dizzy, still trying to get a decent breath of air as she crawled over to Rafi and pulled out the vile that protruded from his chest.

Rafi rolled over and threw up.

"No please," Aldrich cried out. "Just kill me."

"You put your hands on my wife and you killed Valor," Darian's voice was dark with no room for forgiveness. Not for Aldrich.

Cara turned back as Darian lifted Aldrich into the air and brought him down like a long stick over his knee. Aldrich screamed in agony as his back broke.

Darian dropped him to the ground.

The pack arrived coming out of the dark forest.

"He is a traitor," Darian's voice carried over all the snarling, and growling coming from the pack. "He dies a traitor's death."

"No," Aldrich screamed.

Darian stepped back. "Rizer pack, I give him to you to exact justice."

Strong arms wrapped around her, lifting Cara as the forest became a blur all around her. When Darian stopped, they were standing outside Aldrich Town.

Cara stiffened. Her eyes widened as she looked up at him. "I know I shouldn't have gone after Aldrich without you. I'm sorry."

"You're right. You should not have gone after him at all. Now I've broken my promise to you."

Cara shook her head. The desperation and fear in her chest so strong she couldn't draw in air. "I don't care about that. Please don't do this."

Darian gathered her close. "Do what? Cara, what is it?"

"You're leaving me here. You're angry with me."

Darian smoothed back her hair as he shook his head. "Angry yes. But, how could you think I would leave you? Cara, you are my heart. I don't want to live, if it means I have to be without you."

His mouth captured hers in a possessive, deep caress. "You're mine, Cara," he said resting his forehead against hers.

"And you're mine," Cara smiled through the joyful happy tears running down her face. "But, I don't understand why we're here. Why did you bring me back here if not to leave me?"

"You hate this wall. I thought you'd want to see it happen. I thought you'd want to tell everyone they can take it down. Tell them they have nothing to fear from the Rizer pack, as long as they don't hunt wolves."

Cara nodded, as she battled the emotion so strong in her chest she struggled to speak. "I will."

She started toward the water but Darian pulled her back.

"You can't go inside. You're a shifter now. The poison will kill you."

"No, Jules told me that it won't because I haven't shifted."

Darian's face hardened. "She was happy to sacrifice you and get Aldrich in the same token."

Cara frowned as the realization of what would have happened if they'd made it to Aldrich town before Darian could stop them hit her. "I should have listened to you."

"Call out to them," Darian smiled.

Cara nodded and turned toward the wall. "Aldrich Town," she yelled out cupping her hands around her mouth. "Guard on the wall," she tried again.

"Cara?" Her uncle called her name from the guard station. "Is that you?"

"Yes," Cara answered around the emotion that swelled in her chest. "Aldrich is dead. You're free of him. You have to take down the wall."

She could see him now as he leaned out of the guard tower. "The shifters, Cara. It's too dangerous."

"No, it isn't. Aldrich lied to us. They were never after us. Aldrich killed members of the pack. He was hiding inside the town. He made us all serve him. Don't you see?"

She could see the fear on her uncle's face as he relayed the message to the townspeople gathering below him under the tower.

"Cara, there are too many of us that are afraid. We don't know how to live outside the wall anymore. It's safer inside."

"No. You're not even living inside the wall. It's nothing but a cage. You'll be free again. Tell them they'll see the sun, and feel it on their face. Remind them about the waterfall, fresh water, fresh food. They can hunt and the shifters won't come after you as long as you don't kill the wolves."

She watched him holding her breath as he began to relay again to the people below. Darian put his hand at the small of her back, giving her his support.

When her uncle again turned back and the look on his face was strained Cara didn't wait for him to tell her they were still afraid.

"I was afraid too," she called out even louder. "I thought I'd die when I left Aldrich Town. I was terrified. Since I've been gone, I've felt the wind on my face, I've watched the sun rise and set. I found love beyond the wall."

Darian pulled her in close to his side. They waited again. Cara leaned into Darian afraid that they would never bring down the wall. They'd die inside the cage.

She searched her mind trying to find the right thing to say.

"Look," Darian said pointing out toward the guard tower.

Her uncle shoved a loose stone from the top of the wall.

"They're taking it down," Cara whispered, afraid if she said it any louder they might stop. She hugged Darian tighter. They watched all night as stone by stone the wall came down. The poisonous water was buried under the rubble by the time it was finished.

The sun rising illuminated their hopeful faces.

Darian kissed the happy tear that rolled down her face as she looked out at the people who had suffered the cage too.

It was like looking at a memory of the scared young woman she was when she'd escaped and believed she knew all there was to know about love and hate.

Cara didn't feel hate anymore, or fear. There was nothing but happiness and safety welling up inside her as she held onto Darian.

"We're free," she said looking up at her husband.

"What do you mean? You were free, weeks ago."

Cara smiled nuzzling his neck. "I thought so too but, we weren't."

"Cara, what are you saying?"

"You and the pack have been stuck waiting here for Aldrich. He's gone and now-"

"Now we'll live, love, and travel as much as you like."

Cara waited for that feeling she'd lived with for so long to spring up and demand they run as far as their legs could carry them. But it was gone. There was nothing to run from anymore, no need to escape.

"Wherever you are, that's where I want to be."

* * *

THE END

Printed in Great Britain
by Amazon